Naughty

HOUSEWIVES

Naughty
HOUSEWIVES

ELIZABETH SCOTT

NAL
HEAT

NAL Heat
Published by New American Library, a division of
Penguin Group (USA) Inc., 375 Hudson Street,
New York, New York 10014, USA
Penguin Group (Canada), 90 Eglinton Avenue East, Suite 700, Toronto,
Ontario M4P 2Y3, Canada (a division of Pearson Penguin Canada Inc.)
Penguin Books Ltd., 80 Strand, London WC2R 0RL, England
Penguin Ireland, 25 St. Stephen's Green, Dublin 2,
Ireland (a division of Penguin Books Ltd.)
Penguin Group (Australia), 250 Camberwell Road, Camberwell, Victoria 3124,
Australia (a division of Pearson Australia Group Pty. Ltd.)
Penguin Books India Pvt. Ltd., 11 Community Centre, Panchsheel Park,
New Delhi — 110 017, India
Penguin Group (NZ), cnr Airborne and Rosedale Roads, Albany,
Auckland 1310, New Zealand (a division of Pearson New Zealand Ltd.)
Penguin Books (South Africa) (Pty.) Ltd., 24 Sturdee Avenue,
Rosebank, Johannesburg 2196, South Africa

Penguin Books Ltd., Registered Offices:
80 Strand, London WC2R 0RL, England

First published by NAL Heat, an imprint of New American Library,
a division of Penguin Group (USA) Inc.

First Printing, January 2007
10 9 8 7 6 5 4 3 2 1

LIBRARY OF CONGRESS CATALOGING-IN-PUBLICATION DATA

Scott, Elizabeth, 1955–
Naughty housewives/Elizabeth Scott.
p. cm.
ISBN-13: 978-0-451-22038-7
I. Title.
PS3613.A958N38 2007
813'.6—dc22   2006028534

Set in Centaur MT
Designed by Ginger Legato

Printed in the United States of America

To Bill, from his Scheherazade . . .

And for naughty housewives everywhere . . .
and the husbands who love them.

TIT FOR TAT

Chapter One

S helby Stanton stared blindly out the window. The beautifully landscaped yard of her riverfront English Tudor home was immaculate. The terraced banks sloping down to the water were awash in the pinks and whites of azaleas and dogwoods. Spring was bursting into glorious, perfect display. Her marriage was in shambles.

Across the dining room table sat her husband, Eric. He looked as defeated as she felt. They had just returned from their final session with a professional counselor. In the end, and with the therapist's encouragement, Shelby and Eric had both agreed that five years of marriage were too valuable to toss away.

Now they were at an impasse. Business as usual wasn't going to cut it, but neither of them knew quite how to proceed.

Eric had cheated. He'd had a one-night stand with an out-of-town business associate. Unfortunately for Shelby, she hadn't needed the two-hundred-dollar-an-hour head doctor to tell her that there was enough blame to go around. She was well aware of her role in the whole mess.

She was type A to the max, and though she was a full-time homemaker, she'd become more and more involved in her volunteer work, getting busier and busier with each passing week. Though it stuck in her craw to admit it, she'd ignored the warning signs. Eric would cook an elaborate dinner . . . she'd promise to be there, and then show up two hours late. Eric would beg her to get away for a romantic weekend . . . she'd find reason after reason not to go.

It didn't take a rocket scientist to see a recipe for disaster.

Eric had apologized abjectly. She could see the misery in his eyes. Deep inside she felt shame for having treated their marriage with such cavalier disregard. Eric might have cheated physically, but she had let any number of things become more important than her husband, and that was her own fault, not his.

It was time to start over, but she couldn't erase the knot of hurt and anger that gnawed at her gut every time she thought about her husband in bed with another woman. Until she could resolve those feelings, the wounds wouldn't heal.

And try as she might, she'd been able to come up with only one solution.

She laid her hands palms down on the table. She was shaking inside, but refused to show it. She had Eric's attention. His dark brown eyes were solemn as he stared at her face.

She noticed absently that he needed a haircut. His slightly wavy chestnut hair was almost touching his collar. She took a deep breath. "I've made a decision, Eric."

He sat up straighter, as though preparing for a blow. "Okay." His eyes were wary now.

"I realize that we need a fresh start, but I'm still angry. And until I figure out how to get past that, I'm not sure that things are going to improve."

His hands were shoved in his pockets, and he leaned his chair back on two legs, his face grim. "Do you have a suggestion?"

She winced. "I love you, Eric. I'll always love you. But I think I need to sleep with another man."

The legs of his chair hit the floor with a thud. He was on his feet instantly, his hands raking through his hair. His mouth opened and closed three or four times as he started to speak and then changed his mind. The expression on his face was heartbreaking. Revulsion. Anger. Hurt. And finally . . . resignation.

He cleared his throat, not even looking at her when he spoke hoarsely. "If that's what it takes."

She bowed her head, fighting back tears. "Thank you for understanding," she whispered.

She picked up her pocketbook and cell phone. "Don't wait up for me. I'll see you tomorrow."

His head snapped around. "Tonight? You're doing this tonight?" Fury and frustration flashed from his eyes.

She shrugged unhappily. "I want to get it over with."

He shook his head, agitation in every line of his body. "You've already arranged this with some guy you know, haven't you?"

She frowned. "I don't want a relationship, Eric. I'm just looking for a one-night stand. Tit for tat."

He slammed a fist against the wall, causing the chandelier overhead to sway. "For God's sake, Shelby. You can't just go out and get laid."

She lifted her chin, her heart a cold weight in her chest. "Watch me."

Eric waited thirty seconds after the door leading out to the garage closed and then grabbed up his billfold, keys, and cell phone. He would follow her—not to keep tabs on her or to stop her or to find out who the guy was, but to keep her safe.

God, just thinking about Shelby cruising for a guy made his stomach turn. In many ways his pretty, driven wife was naive. She'd only ever slept with one man besides her husband. Would she think about condoms and diseases? Did she know about

date-rape drugs? His hands were shaking, and he cursed his own stupidity.

One lousy, stupid mistake. That was all it took. He'd been a fool for one lonely, reckless evening, and now his life was shot to hell. He hadn't even been out of the woman's bed before he knew he'd made the worst error of his life. He'd cheated on his wife, the person he loved more than anyone or anything in the world.

It didn't matter that Shelby might have been to blame for their emotional distance. Nothing excused his own appalling behavior, and he was damned lucky he still had a wife and a marriage. It might take months, even years to repair the damage, but he would make it up to her.

He had to.

He followed her at a careful distance. Her little silver Mazda was easy to spot. The sun had gone down, and streetlights were popping on. As darkness fell, it seemed that Shelby drove aimlessly, finally ending up on the campus of the nearby university. She paused in front of a large dorm that housed a lot of the athletes.

His stomach clenched. Hell, no. Some things were just too dangerous.

She must have arrived at the same conclusion, because she put the car in gear and moved on. She wound from street to street, crossing from one block to the next. Finally she ended up on the infamous strip where small restaurants and bars catered to the college crowd.

He watched from a distance as she parked and got out. Her silvery-blond hair curled at her shoulders, and her long, beautiful legs were eye-catching even from far away. He imagined her hazel eyes would be wide. She wouldn't find this easy. He knew her that well.

She wore a fuchsia spandex top and a slim black skirt. At their earlier appointment, Shelby had worn a dignified charcoal gray blazer, but now she had ditched the top layer and was dressed like a woman ready for some action.

She entered Down the Hatch, a dark, smoky, pub-style eatery. Hot wings and longneck beers were the house specialties. On weekends, aspiring musicians held court on a small stage. It was a typical college hangout.

He peered in the front window and saw Shelby approach the bar. She climbed up on a stool, flashing quite a bit of leg in the process.

With her back to him, he felt pretty safe. The place had fifteen or twenty tables. He chose a small one in a dimly lit corner near the john and not in his wife's line of vision. Not that she was looking around. She had already ordered a drink.

Despite his mood, he had to grin. Shelby hated beer. She was nursing a seltzer water. He ordered a Heineken and settled back to see what happened. Part of him expected her to chicken out. Or maybe hoped she would.

This had to be the most bizarre and painful night of his marriage to date. But perhaps inevitable. Shelby was competitive

in everything she did, be it racquetball or business. It wasn't entirely surprising that she'd chosen this course of action to even the score.

And she was an inveterate list maker. Write it down . . . check it off. Focused and goal-oriented . . . that was his wife. He wouldn't be surprised if somewhere in the depths of the pink Kate Spade clutch he'd bought her for Valentine's Day was a scrap of paper: *1) Put marriage troubles behind me, 2) Fuck a stranger, 3) Forgive Eric.*

Some women might have gone behind his back. Not Shelby. She was forthright and honest to a fault. In her younger days, she had even been accused of not having any tact. She'd learned to temper her remarks with a modicum of forethought, but guile wasn't part of her makeup.

Nor had it ever been part of his. He could probably have kept Shelby from ever discovering his indiscretion. Deception had dangled the tempting apple for a split second. But regret and remorse had forced him into an almost immediate confession. Telling her what he had done was the hardest thing he had ever had to do. Seeing the stunned hurt on her face was a punishment of its own.

But he had a feeling that his painful journey to reconciliation was far from over.

Shelby knew almost immediately that Eric was following her. And she knew why. He was one of those guys who had it programmed in their DNA to be protective of women. Eric always made sure the oil in her car was changed and her tires were rotated. She never had to pump her own gas. He was adamant about her keeping her cell phone charged in case of an emergency.

For a moment she thought guiltily about how many evenings she had driven home late, some of those in bad weather. Had Eric been worried about her each and every time? Some husbands would have been paranoid and jealous of the long hours she put in at various charity events. Not Eric. He trusted her. He loved her. She knew that beyond the shadow of a doubt.

Which had made his infidelity such a blow.

She frowned and slammed the lid on those unpleasant memories. With a pained sigh, she sipped her drink and surreptitiously scoped out the patrons seated near her. It didn't take her five minutes to decide that screwing a college guy wasn't going to happen. They all looked like children. Not that thirty-one was ancient, but good Lord, she would feel like scum.

So maybe a grad student. She eyed the bartender. He was older . . . mid-twenties at least. And his eyes held experience and maturity. At least she wouldn't be imagining his mother's shocked face if the guy ended up in her bed.

It was a Wednesday night. Things weren't too busy. Occasionally Bar Guy spoke to her . . . a comment about the great weather. An offer of pretzels. A reference to the recent national title won by the women's basketball team.

He wasn't really flirting. Just doing his job. Maybe trying to pass the time during a long shift.

She uncrossed her legs and wrapped her ankles around the rungs of the stool. She was nervous as a cat. Alcohol might have helped, but she was a cheap drunk, and she needed her wits about her tonight.

She swapped the water for a Diet Coke and waited until the two guys seated nearest her carried their drinks to a table. Now her end of the bar was deserted.

She couldn't analyze this to death. She just had to do it. She straightened her spine and thrust out her boobs. They fell somewhere between Kate Moss and Dolly Parton. Well, if she were being truthful . . . more to the Kate end of the spectrum.

Bar Guy had a rag in his hand and was wiping up spilled tequila. He wasn't looking at her.

She inhaled and pasted a smile on her face. In the mirror behind the bar, she looked more petrified than seductive. *Oh, hell . . .*

She spoke softly, not wanting to be overheard. "Do you have a girlfriend?"

Bar Guy froze for half a second, and then his head came up. His gaze met hers . . . veiled surprise on his end . . . what she hoped was coyness on hers.

He tossed the rag in the sink. "Nope."

His eyes were light blue with a hint of green around the pupils, probably emphasized by the T-shirt he wore. His dark blond hair was cut military short. He had a nice body. He was maybe an inch taller than Eric, but where Eric was broad through the shoulders and chest, this guy was leaner and lankier. Eric had played college football. Bar Guy would look comfortable swinging a baseball bat.

He wasn't really her type. But did that matter? No. Without standing up on her toes and peeking over the bar, she couldn't really see his crotch. She assumed he had all the necessary equipment.

When he didn't pick up the conversational ball, she continued. "Are you straight?"

His eyes narrowed. "Yep."

"What time do you get off work?"

Long pause. She could feel heat rising from her throat to her face.

He cocked his head. "In thirty minutes. I came in early today for the lunch crowd."

Her hands were starting to shake, so she tucked them under her thighs. "Are you a student?" She wasn't sure why it was important. Having the guy's life history didn't make this any easier.

He nodded at a man down the bar and took him a refill. Seconds later he was back. "I'm doing a doctoral program in anthropology."

He wasn't smiling. She wondered if that was a bad sign.

Bar Guy glanced at her left hand. "You're married."

"Yes." She felt her flush deepen.

He raised an eyebrow in silent inquiry.

"My husband cheated on me. I'm evening the score."

"That could get you in trouble," he said quietly.

"He knows."

Incredulity etched his face. "No shit."

She shrugged. "I need to be able to move on. This will help. And it's a long story. I wasn't completely blameless," she admitted. For some reason, she didn't want him to think badly of Eric.

He shook his head. "I think you're crazy, pretty lady. But I'm not stupid. Give me a few more minutes and I can clock out."

It was more like twenty. She counted. And each agonizing sixty-second chunk lasted a lifetime.

When Bar Guy appeared beside her on her side of the bar, she trembled. "Ready?" Her voice came out as an embarrassing squeak.

He nodded without speaking. Outside, they each paused simultaneously. Shelby cleared her throat. "Your place okay?"

He shook his head. "I live with three other guys. I wouldn't recommend it. How about your house?"

"No," she said simply. "I guess we'll go down the street."

It was a balmy night. They walked to the generic chain motel on the next block. It catered to alums visiting campus for sporting events. The squat two-story building was just short of an eyesore. Someone had planted purple petunias in a narrow flower bed out front. If the flowers were supposed to offset the effect of the unadorned utilitarian structure, they failed.

Shelby walked right up to the front desk and plunked down her credit card in exchange for two plastic key cards. Bar Guy had accompanied her in silence, shoulder to shoulder, but not touching her. Outside, in the harsh glare of the streetlights, he seemed older, more dangerous. By the time they were inside room 107 with the door closed, she was close to hyperventilating.

Eric parked in the shadows as far away from a streetlight as he could get. He watched Shelby and her escort enter and then leave the lobby. The guy seemed harmless, but so did your average serial killer.

The motel had no inside corridors. All the rooms opened directly onto the parking lot. He saw his wife and the man she had just met go in. Through a gap in the curtains, he saw a light click on. And then an unseen hand pulled the curtains together.

His head dropped back against the seat and he groaned. God, how long would this take? Anguished emotions buffeted him, one after another. Jealousy. Regret. Fear. It was all he could do to keep from jumping out of the car, pounding on the damned door, and dragging Shelby out by the hair.

Would the guy be gentle with her, or was he some jerk who would take what he wanted and leave her hanging?

His hands, which had been gripping the steering wheel, fell to his lap. His chest was tight; his stomach churned; his eyes burned.

He tried to imagine what was happening in there behind that

closed door. Was Shelby undressing for the guy ... slowly and so damned sexily ... the way she did for him?

His cock stirred and flexed, and he felt the lash of shame and embarrassment. Shelby would kill him if she knew he was getting aroused.

But the rush of feelings snowballed, washing over him like a tidal wave, leaving him taut and hungry. He closed his eyes and he could see every inch of her slender, shapely body. Her small, perfect tits, her narrow waist, her fluff of baby-fine pussy hair.

Trembling, he unzipped his pants and lifted his cock free. It was already rock hard, the eye oozing moisture even as his heart wept for what was happening behind those curtains.

He stroked his length once ... twice. He would just hold himself ... a little pressure—that was all. Anything else would be unforgivable.

Behind his closed eyelids an erotic cinema unfolded. Shelby nude and lovely against cheap sheets. Shelby sliding her tongue into Bar Guy's mouth. Shelby straddling Bar Guy's waist. Shelby's pink lips closing around a strange man's dick. Shelby crying out in ecstasy as a long, thick penis penetrated her, filled her up, drove her mad.

Choking and gasping, he dragged angrily at his unruly prick, wanting to punish it for its foray into a faceless woman's bed. For its entirely inappropriate reaction to his wife's sexual exploits. For making it so damned difficult for his brain to function.

His fingers clenched around his aching flesh. Up and down,

harder and faster, in a rhythm as familiar as his own face in the mirror. He whispered her name, felt her warm, supple legs circle his waist, her soft, sweet breasts pillow against his chest.

He reached lower for his balls, tugging at them, wincing at the restrictive cloth that bound them. Shards of fire swept from his scrotum to his shaft. The movie played in his head . . . an endless reel, frame after frame of torture. *Shelby.* The soundless cry clogged his throat. His spine arched, and hot come erupted.

Almost insensate, he slumped against the seat belt, spent . . . exhausted . . . tormented.

When he could breathe normally, he lifted his arm and looked at his watch. Fifteen minutes had passed.

It was going to be a hell of a long night. . . .

Chapter Two

Shelby leaned her back against the closed door and looked around the small room, mentally cataloging its contents. The decor was vintage mid-eighties, and no doubt the dark nondescript carpet hid a multitude of sins. The minimal accoutrements were predictable. Generic framed art over two double beds. A beige plastic phone beside a Gideon Bible. Slick polyester bedspreads in a ghastly amber-and-orange floral motif.

Bar Guy stood silently on the opposite side of the room. His arms hung loosely by his sides. His face was expressionless, but his sharp eyes watched her intently. Finally, he tossed his lightweight denim jacket on a chair. "I'm going to clean up."

She felt her knees turn to spaghetti. "Don't you want to

know my name?" she said, half piqued at his deliberate lack of interest.

The whisper of a smile tilted his lips and then vanished. "Do you want me to know your name?"

"It's Shelby," she said defiantly.

After a pregnant moment, he gave a brief nod and turned toward the bathroom.

"Wait," she said, feeling the encounter slipping beyond her control. "What's yours?"

He laid a hand high on the frame of the door leading into the bathroom and hung his head, looking down at his feet. "Does it matter?"

The implied criticism stung. She didn't make a practice of seducing and screwing strange men. Although in all fairness, Bar Guy didn't know that. She shrugged unhappily. "I think it does."

Still not looking at her. A long, disgusted sigh. "Jason." And then he disappeared and shut the door, leaving her to dangle in frantic indecision.

She dithered for at least a minute. Should she strip and get in bed? Would it be better to let him undress her? Eric liked to do that.

Before she could come up with a plan, Jason was back after having taken what surely must have been the shortest shower on record. She sucked in a startled breath. He was nude except for the thin white motel towel tucked around his hips. The minimal

covering tented in front, leaving no doubt as to his readiness. His skin was lightly tanned...his chest dusted with golden hair.

He cocked his head toward the bathroom, his expression inscrutable. "Your turn."

On unsteady legs she walked past him, inhaling the not unpleasant scent of motel soap and male skin. At the last instant she grabbed his denim jacket from the chair. She had to have some kind of robe. She'd never survive walking back into that room buck naked.

Her shower lasted a bit longer than his. She tucked her hair in a tiny shower cap and wished she had a razor to shave her legs. Then she gave herself a figurative smack. *Come on, Shelby.* Did it really matter what this guy thought of her?

She dried off and slipped into his jacket. It hit her just below the butt, barely covering up the essentials. The faint odor of cigarette smoke and aftershave clung to the fabric. One quick glance in the mirror was hardly reassuring. She looked like Joan of Arc on the way to the stake.

She opened the door. The bedroom was dimly lit. Jason had extinguished all the lights except for a small lamp near the window. He was reclining on top of the nearest bed, the spread still in place, as was his towel. He held the TV remote, and although the sound was muted, he was surfing the cable channels. What was it about men and their remotes?

He turned off the TV as soon as she appeared. She hovered

in the doorway, her heart pounding in her chest with sickening thuds. Her bare legs felt cold and exposed. She tugged the lapels of the jacket closer together and forced herself to walk toward the bed.

Jason stood up. "Am I supposed to take charge, or is this your call?"

She nibbled her bottom lip, her nipples puckering beneath the rough denim. "Why don't we let nature take its course?" she said quietly, trying to sound calm and reasonable when her mind was skittering in a million different directions.

He walked toward her, then lifted a hand and touched her cheek. Her skin tightened and her breathing quickened. She sensed rather than saw him remove the towel. She was afraid to look down.

He bent his head. Their lips met. His kiss was nice, just the right amount of pressure. She couldn't seem to respond. Her body felt like ice.

He lifted her hands to his shoulders. "Relax, Shelby," he muttered, his voice husky. His arms went around her, and she felt his erection brush against her thighs. A dribble of moisture smeared her leg.

She hiccuped a breath and moaned when his tongue slid inside her mouth. He tasted different, alien. But not in a bad way. Her tongue met his hesitantly, and she felt his cock move against her.

His arms were bands of steel. It struck her suddenly that he

could overpower her with little effort at all. Uneasiness slithered in her belly, and she stiffened involuntarily.

His hands slid down her back to cup her ass. "Is this really what you want?" He sighed, his breath hot against her ear.

He had gone still. She trembled violently, wondering if she had made a mistake. But it was far too late to back out now. "Yes," she whispered, pressing closer into his embrace. "I want you."

He didn't need another invitation. One hand came up to fist in her hair, and the other dragged her limp form flush against his body. She slid her arms around his waist, feeling muscle and sinew.

It was his turn to tremble, and his harsh words of praise ripped open a hidden chamber of emotion. Moisture, her own this time, gathered between her thighs, and she felt the slow, liquid river of arousal steal through her veins.

He kissed her again, ravenously, roughly. His hands were under the jacket now, cupping her breasts, thumbing the nipples with firm pressure. She whimpered, feeling the hot length of his cock between them, craving it . . . needing it inside her.

He bit the side of her neck, the flash of pain burying itself deep in her pussy. "Oh, God . . ."

He growled and tilted her head back, raking his teeth from her throat down her chest to one aching nipple. He sucked it deep into his mouth, and she shrieked as a stunning climax wrenched through her.

He scooped her into his arms and turned toward the bed. He ripped back the covers with one hand and lowered her beneath him.

With her last functioning brain cell, she groaned out a question: "Condom?"

He reached into the pocket of the jacket she wore and jerked out a foil packet.

"Thank God."

He supported her shoulders and ripped off the jacket, leaving her nude and open to his gaze. He paused a moment to look his fill, and the reverence in his gaze as his palm skated over her skin from breast to hip was balm to her shredded nerves.

He kissed her navel. "You are one damned beautiful woman, Shelby. Your husband must be an idiot. It makes me ache just to look at you."

But he was through looking. He tore open the condom packet and sheathed himself. Quickly he moved between her thighs. She felt the big head of his penis probe at her sex, and a shocked cry ripped from her throat as he shoved deep in one forceful motion.

She dragged his mouth down for a kiss, feeling the imminent onslaught of another orgasm. A voice in her head cried, *"Shame,"* for allowing a strange man to arouse her so quickly and thoroughly. But finer emotions were not part of this elemental joining.

This was raw sex. Pure and simple.

He shuddered in her arms, clearly trying to last. He dropped his forehead to hers. "Sorry," he ground out between clenched teeth. "It's been a while."

He moved slowly, in and out, and they moaned in unison. The slide of flesh on flesh was almost painful in its intensity.

He nipped her earlobe. "Are you close?"

She nodded blindly, tilting her hips to drive him deeper. He reached between their joined bodies and found her clit, pinching it softly.

She jerked and exploded in heat and fire. He shuddered and rammed his cock to the hilt, sending shock waves rattling through her climax. Dimly, she heard him shout as he thrust again and again and again until he jerked, cried out, and found his release.

She might have dozed. She wasn't sure. The stress in her life in recent days meant she slept poorly and woke up tired.

The man who had rolled off her was now sprawled at her side, his chest still heaving with jerky breaths. She wanted to touch him, but it seemed awkward and too familiar.

He left the bed, and she heard water running in the bathroom. Moments later he returned and, sitting beside her, used a warm washrag to dab gently at her swollen flesh.

The terry cloth against her supersensitive nerve endings made her wince. His hand moving between her legs felt more intimate than anything they had done so far. Ripples of remembered pleasure continued to pulsate in her sex. She was still aroused, ready to do it all over again. But that would be cheating.

Doggedly, and with no small amount of regret, she forced herself to speak. "You can go now."

He tossed the rag aside and lay down beside her, propping up on one elbow. "I don't think so." His eyes were hooded, his expression difficult to read. His fingers plucked at her nearest nipple until it tightened into a raspberry bud.

Surprise and excitement dried her throat. "Do we have another condom?"

His grin made everything that was feminine inside her clench with helpless longing.

"Doesn't matter," he said simply. And in one graceful move he knelt over her chest. He took his cock in his hand, working it with knowledgeable strokes until it quickly came to life. He was thicker and wider than Eric, though not quite as long. His heavy balls brushed her breasts.

She found herself mesmerized by the tautly erect penis bobbing in front of her eyes. The vein on the underside stood out in stark relief to the dark red color. It was beautiful, really. She wondered if all men's cocks were as varied and wonderfully different as Jason's and Eric's. Her one other basis for comparison was long ago and soon forgotten.

He swallowed hard, obviously trying to keep control of the situation. He touched her cheek with his free hand. "You're incredible, Shelby. Any man would be lucky to have you."

He spoke the words quietly, like a vow. His simple pronounce-
ment touched her deeply, and she felt a tingle of shame that this
stranger's approval should mean so much to her.

She couldn't watch any longer. She shivered hard, almost
afraid of this stark eroticism.

His husky voice broke the silence. "Look at me, Shelby." It
was a command, a dominant male claiming what he wanted.

She obeyed like a puppet, snared in a silken noose of arousal.
Her hands came up to caress his taut, muscled buttocks.

He continued to play with himself. The tip of his penis
yielded one pearly drop of come. Faster and faster his fingers
moved. His head went back. His eyes squeezed shut. With a
hoarse shout, and holding his cock clenched in his right hand, he
shot come on her breasts. He came forever, it seemed, and when
he was finished, his cock was still partially erect.

His cheeks were flushed. His eyes glittered. He fell onto his
back beside her with an incoherent murmur, breathing heavily.
His big hand played idly with her hair. After a moment he
found the washcloth and ran it over her skin with painstaking
care.

She had come twice, and still her sex hummed with energy.
She moved against him like a cat, wishing she dared touch herself down there. As if he had read her mind, his hand moved between her thighs and he began to stroke her.

She stared at him in confusion. "Again?"

His cocky smile and hot eyes challenged her to complain.

"We're not done yet, honey. Not by a long shot." He startled her when he moved suddenly and slid down in the bed. His large palms cupped her thighs and slid them apart. And then his tongue zeroed in on her pleasure spot like a heat-seeking missile. He licked and flicked and suckled with fanatical attention to detail. She made embarrassing noises, unable to help herself as she writhed and jerked in his grasp.

Occasionally he used two long fingers to thrust inside her swollen pussy, probing gently at her sensitive flesh and making her squirm.

She panted, too horny to be bashful. "Use your teeth," she whispered brokenly.

He raked her clit with his teeth, thrusting roughly and rhythmically with three fingers now. Pressure built in her womb. She arched her back, seeking blindly for what was just out of reach. And then he rotated his thumb on her clit, pressed down, and held her as she shattered in his arms.

They slept like exhausted children in a tangle of arms and legs. Shelby dreamed . . . disturbing, erotic visions of cocks and lips and hard, masculine chests.

When she awoke, she was disoriented. She glanced at the digital readout glowing from the clock on the bedside table: three a.m.

She touched his shoulder, absently noting the pleasing combination of bone and skin. "Jason, I have to go." Her whisper

sounded loud in the silent room, but she had a sudden craving to be back in her bed at home.

He groaned and rolled to his back, simultaneously lifting her with strong arms to sit on top of him. Her pussy rested against his balls. As she watched, his cock began to rise.

She frowned. "We don't have a condom," she reminded him.

A long, pregnant pause.

He grimaced, his eyes squeezing shut. "I can go get one."

She shook her head, feeling the weight of common sense and responsibility drag her down. "I think I really have to go."

They dressed in silence. He handed her a shoe. She helped him find a missing sock. When they were fully clothed, she gave him the two key cards and picked up her pocketbook. "Will you please turn these in at the office when I'm gone?"

He frowned. "You know what they'll think."

Shelby's reply was as bleak as her heart felt. "Then they'd be right . . . wouldn't they?"

He pulled her into his arms. "I won't forget you, Shelby . . . woman with no last name. I may become a priest and give up sex entirely. It will never be the same after tonight."

His gentle teasing comforted her somehow. She nuzzled his shoulder with her cheek. "Thank you for this. It might have been awful with someone else."

He looked down at her. "And with me?" Perhaps he didn't realize the hint of vulnerability she heard in his voice.

She touched his cheek, her heart contracting. "You were amazing. I won't forget you either."

And then she reached for the doorknob and her old life.

Eric jerked awake when he heard the door open. He'd been in and out of an uneasy doze for hours.

A couple appeared in the doorway and stepped onto the sidewalk. He saw Shelby rub her arms in the chilly night air. Bar Guy tried to offer her his jacket, but she refused.

And then Eric's whole world threatened to come crashing down around his ears. Bar Guy leaned down to kiss Shelby on the cheek. A knot gathered in Eric's belly. The knot grew to watermelon size when his pretty wife hesitated a split second and then went up on tiptoe to kiss the damned man full on the mouth, her hands cupping his face. The guy's arms came around her, practically lifting her off her feet.

Eric couldn't watch anymore. His fingers were numb on the steering wheel. He put the gearshift in drive and gently eased toward the driveway.

It didn't matter. The couple in front of room 107 was oblivious to his presence.

He drove home on autopilot, taking every shortcut and back road to beat Shelby home. At least, he hoped like hell she was coming home. *Please, God, let her be coming home.*

The streets were empty in the predawn hours. He made it to their driveway in record time. He parked in the garage and lowered

the door. He was in their bedroom stripping off his clothes when he heard her climbing the stairs.

He dove into bed and pulled the covers beneath his chin.

Shelby entered the room like a ghost, her soft footsteps barely making a sound. There was a brief rustle in the bathroom, and then she slid into bed beside him with a sigh.

Eric's stomach clenched. He could smell the other man's scent in her hair and on her skin.

She lay motionless beside him, but the physical and emotional chasm between them was nothing new. Ever since he had confessed his momentary fall from grace, they'd shared this big king-size bed in stony silence.

His hands and feet were icy cold. He wanted to touch her so badly he had to clench his fists in the covers. What was she thinking? What had she done? Not knowing was tearing him apart.

She shifted onto her side with another little sigh, and he lost it. He simply lost it.

With a ragged curse, he scooted across the mattress and dragged her into his arms, tucking her spoon-fashion against his chest.

She cried out in surprise, but she didn't protest or try to evade his touch.

Eric groaned. She felt so soft and warm in his arms. He'd almost forgotten what it was like to hold her. He buried his face in her hair. His cock, erect and ready as it had been on and off all night, nuzzled against her pert bottom, desperate to know his wife's pussy again. He tried to communicate his desperation. His plea for forgiveness. His deep need to make love to his wife and know that things were the way they used to be.

But even as he was marshaling his arguments, preparing his request for absolution in light of the new circumstances, he realized that his aching prick would go at least another night without relief.

His lovely, sexy, well-fucked wife was sound asleep in his arms.

Chapter Three

E ric couldn't face her the following morning. He'd barely slept, caught between a desperate aching arousal and the equally insistent fear that Shelby had found release and satisfaction in the arms of another man.

She slept like the dead, and as the first hints of dawn streaked the sky, she never even moved when he slid out of bed. He showered and dressed automatically, his mind assessing and discarding one possible scenario after another.

He wanted to hear everything that had happened behind that motel door last night. Desperately. Beyond reason. Not knowing was tearing him apart.

But a nasty little voice inside his head kept whispering that some things were best kept in the dark. Ignored. Pushed under the rug. Any damned cliché you cared to name as a justification for sheer cowardly avoidance.

When he was ready for work, he picked up his gym bag and stood by the bed. God, she was beautiful. She slept deeply, so still and quiet he could barely see the rise and fall of her chest. Her face was relaxed and peaceful. One breast was exposed above the sheet. He trembled, and his hands clenched into fists.

He wanted to touch her, stroke her to wakefulness, plunge his cock deep inside her warm, welcoming body and demand his husbandly rights.

Ha. That was a misnomer. Any rights he'd ever laid claim to had been annulled well and good by his stupid screwing around. But now, in one wild and impetuous evening, Shelby had evened the score.

Or had she?

He still felt guilty as hell for cheating on her. He still didn't know how to go about patching up his marriage. He still was disgusted with himself for getting off on the idea of a stranger fucking his wife.

Impasse.

He stepped back from the bed and took a deep breath. Distance. That was what he needed. Distance. And the chance to sort out his feelings.

Maybe even Shelby needed some time to let what had happened last night seep into her psyche. Would she look at him

differently tonight? Would their marriage be back on track? Would she be the same woman?

The sheer number of unanswered questions buzzing around in his head made him nauseous. With a helpless curse, he spun on his heel and walked away from temptation. A punishing workout and a long day on the job might give him a chance to regain his equilibrium. And if not ... well ... he and Shelby would hash things out tonight, once and for all.

Shelby rolled over with a groan and looked at the clock. Ten a.m. *Good Lord.* She hadn't slept this late since last year, when she had the flu. Come to think of it, some of her symptoms were similar. Aches in unusual places. A stomach that pitched and rolled. A vicious headache.

She sat up with a wince and looked around the bedroom. Eric was gone. Not that his absence was anything unusual. It was Thursday, a regular workday. No reason at all why he should still be in bed or even in the house. Just because everything in her world seemed changed beyond measure was no reason for him to be equally distraught. And just because he was gone didn't mean it was a reaction to last night.

He woke up and went to work. Like he did every day. End of story.

So why did the deafening silence in their comfortable, familiar home seem loud with unspoken accusation? Why was the vision of his disapproving gaze locked in her anxious brain?

She stumbled into the bathroom, avoiding the sight of herself in the mirror. She didn't want to know what she looked like. In the shower, she turned the water as hot as she dared, scrubbing her body with vicious strokes, trying to eradicate the lingering effects of last night's sexual antics.

Guilt lay like a pall on her shoulders. Not for having a one-night stand. She and Eric had agreed on that. It was strictly necessary.

But the fact that she had been able to be aroused by another man . . . the fact that she had reveled in the sheer carnal pleasure of hot, meaningless sex with a stranger, made her squirm with shame. At least Eric's fling had been a momentary indiscretion driven by male lust, and somewhat understandable given the circumstances.

Her brief encounter was supposed to be something she endured. Something vaguely distasteful that gave her closure. She wasn't supposed to enjoy it, and she certainly wasn't supposed to contemplate what it would be like to do it again.

She clapped a hand over her mouth, trembling from head to toe as water sluiced over her in what should have been a cleansing waterfall. *Oh, God.* The unbelievable truth stunned her. She was thinking about having sex with Bar Guy again. Bar Guy naked beside her in bed. On top of her, behind her, thrusting between her legs with wild abandon. Bar Guy . . .

No, that wasn't right. His name was Jason. Quiet, good-with-his-hands Jason.

And she had used Jason the bar guy quite deliberately. Okay, so maybe he had enjoyed it. But that didn't excuse her behavior.

She could stay in the shower until her skin turned pruny, but all the water in the world wouldn't erase the guilt she felt.

She loved Eric. She adored him. And even though it killed her to know he had screwed another woman, nothing could erase the bond Shelby knew would always exist with her handsome husband.

She paused a moment to think about his infidelity. It still made her sad, but the sharp stab of anger had all but disappeared. Replaced, if the truth were told, by the enormity of what she had just admitted to herself. Did she dare admit it to Eric as well?

They had a marriage built on understanding and trust. Eric could have hidden his infidelity, but he didn't. Even though he took the risk of alienating her completely, he'd been man enough to confess his mistake.

She, on the other hand, in all her angry, righteous superiority, had mistakenly demanded restitution. She had made Eric the villain. But it hadn't taken her long at all to do something far more foolish and potentially more destructive.

She'd had a chance to be the bigger person. Especially knowing her own culpability in the situation, she could have forgiven Eric his onetime mistake, no matter how hurtful. She could have put their marriage and their lives back on track.

But instead, she'd insisted she needed to even the score.

This time, as she dried her body with a fluffy mauve towel, she gazed long and hard at her reflection in the mirror. Her eyes were dark with confusion, her cheeks flushed with mortification.

Her lower lip trembled as she stared at her bare breasts, the gentle curve of her stomach, the neatly trimmed blond fluff of curls between her legs. She remembered the hot touch of Jason's gaze as he saw her nude body for the first time. She remembered how much his murmured words of appreciation and praise had stroked her feminine vanity, just as his sure hands stroked her sensitive skin. Her nipples tightened, and her breathing grew shallow. She would give anything in the world to have Eric here beside her right now.

Eric could help her make some sense of this confusing mishmash of feelings. And she was beginning to see an ugly possibility.

Perhaps last night had not been about revenge or evening the score at all. Perhaps her stated reasons had been nothing more than a pretext to hide the unpalatable truth.

Was it possible that she had used Eric's cheating as an excuse to experiment in a way she had only fantasized about? The frightening reality settled in her stomach like a stone. Was she actually glad her husband had given her the opportunity to do something she would never have dared do in ordinary circumstances?

She'd seduced another man. She had enjoyed it. And the naughty, uncensored, wanton woman inside of her yearned to do it again.

She dressed automatically in khakis and a beige cotton sweater. The bland clothes fit her mood. She wanted to blend into the background. She was afraid that if she let her guard down, a huge scarlet A would appear on her chest, telling the whole world what she had done last night in a seedy hotel room on the strip.

She couldn't stomach breakfast, and besides, it was almost lunchtime now. She glanced automatically at the calendar on the kitchen counter. That calendar was her bible. It kept track of all the many ways she contributed to the community. She had been proud of that calendar. At least, until she contemplated how her overcommitment had pushed Eric away. How her whirlwind of "important" activities had ignored his needs.

Why had she done it? Was praise from outsiders really more important than her marriage? Self-esteem had always been an issue for her. Growing up in foster care could do that to you. But she hadn't recognized her total absorption in her busy calendar for what it was, even though Eric had begged time and again for her attention. She was so ashamed of having failed him as a wife. And she wanted to make it up to him.

But it would be difficult. They hadn't had sex in over two months. Intimacy seemed scary and unattainable. Especially if she were honest about last night. She hadn't a clue how Eric would react.

She picked up the phone and begged off from the two meetings she had scheduled for the afternoon. Then she went about planning a romantic dinner for two that would set the stage for reconciliation sex. Did one of her Martha Stewart cookbooks have a menu for something like that? Stifling a slightly hysterical giggle, she sat down on a stool at the counter and began an extensive grocery list.

Eric discovered that a forty-five-minute weight-training workout and a grueling eight-hour day behind a piled-up desk did nothing to diminish a hard-on. He was surprised that no one had called him on his total lack of concentration that day.

He was entitled to a damn Oscar for his performance. Best Screwed-up Man in a Non–Leading Man Role. They should definitely add that category. Think how many contenders there would be. Another man had fucked his wife last night.

At five o'clock he closed his office door and rested his elbows on his desk, his head in his hands. He was scared to go home. Scared that her face would still be distant and unwelcoming. Scared that she might not even be home at all.

God, he was losing his mind. All he could think about was seeing his wife standing in a pool of light, kissing a stranger. Strangely enough, thinking of the two of them in bed wasn't what hurt the most. It was the memory of her slender hand touching the guy's cheek, that simple, evocative gesture that spoke of intimacy and tenderness. Every time he thought of it, he went crazy with a tornado of emotions.

He still carried a shitload of guilt. Regret for not having been

able to reach her when she started pulling away. And now anger. At her. At himself. At some dumb-ass stranger who was lucky enough to have been in the right place at the right time.

He gathered his things wearily and headed for the parking garage. He'd contemplated stopping for flowers, but the gesture seemed empty and trite. He and Shelby were way beyond healing a rift with simple gestures and meaningless gifts.

He drove through the university on the way home. It wasn't even out of his way. It was a stupid, pointless, deliberately self-punishing move, but he pulled into the parking lot of the motel and stared at the all-too-familiar door. If he went inside, would he be able to smell her perfume lingering in the air? Would the sex have left its mark somehow?

Eight hours away from his pretty wife had done nothing to tame the beast raging inside him. He was losing control. And he couldn't do a damn thing about it. He felt like one of those werewolf creatures, tortured and writhing as they changed form. He didn't even know the man inside him clawing to get out.

Normal, even-tempered Eric had been left behind somewhere. The creature behind the wheel, seething with anger and lust and anguished self-doubt, was a frightening stranger. But that stranger was firmly in the driver's seat.

When he walked into the house, the first thing that assaulted his senses was the smell of cinnamon and baked apples. He paused, minutely soothed by the mouthwatering aroma. Shelby knew he loved apple pie, and hers were the best he had ever tasted.

He dropped his briefcase, keys, and cell phone on the small side table in the foyer and followed his nose to the kitchen. He paused in the doorway, striving for calm. The XM radio was set to a classical station, and the plaintive sound of violins and flutes filled the air.

Shelby had her back to him, rinsing a bowl in the sink. She was wearing a flirty, silky yellow skirt with a yellow-and-blue-striped cotton peasant blouse.

Her shoulders and legs were lightly tanned, and she wore simple leather sandals on her feet. He'd bet his last dime that she tasted even better than the pie.

It struck him suddenly to wonder if the baked offering was in the line of the flowers he had decided not to buy. He sniffed further and identified roast beef and something else, a vegetable maybe, with cheese in it. Two baked potatoes sat cooling on the stovetop.

He cleared his throat. "Shelby?"

She jumped visibly, and the spoon she was holding clattered in the sink. Her hand went to her throat. "Eric, I didn't hear you come in."

She flushed bright red, and then the color faded, leaving her looking pale and anxious. He frowned. She didn't exactly seem happy to see him despite the elaborate meal. She hadn't been happy to see him in a long time. It hurt, but he kept his expression impassive.

He leaned a hip against the counter. "Something smells good."

That coaxed a tiny smile from her. "It's almost ready. Do you want some wine?"

He took the hint and opened a bottle of their favorite merlot. He poured two glasses and carried hers across the room. It almost seemed as though she flinched when he reached her side. He noticed that she was careful not to let their fingers touch at all as she took the goblet from him.

He sipped his drink slowly, not moving away. For some odd reason, he found that he liked making her nervous. She drained her glass in two gulps and went back to washing the same bowl.

She spoke again, not facing him, her voice tremulous. "If you want to watch the first part of the news, I'll call you when it's on the table."

He stepped behind her, his rigid cock brushing the folds of her skirt. "What's with the Suzy Homemaker routine?" he growled, unreasonably irritated by her meekness. "You know we always work on fixing dinner together."

She slipped past him and crossed to the stove, bending to remove a bubbling casserole from the oven and then putting it on a hot pad. "Well, I was in the mood to cook. That's all."

She straightened, still not meeting his eyes, and poured herself another glass of wine. "I tried a new broccoli casserole recipe."

"Fuck dinner."

The fragile crystal stem slipped from her fingers and shattered at her feet, spraying glass and burgundy liquid everywhere.

He cursed beneath his breath. "Don't move." Her thin sandals were little protection against flying debris. He lifted her in his arms and carried her to a stool. Several tiny slivers of glass glinted against her skin. He extracted them gently, trying not to notice her leg pressed against his shoulder.

He removed her sandals and carefully inspected each foot. Her graceful arches struck him as unbearably erotic. He took a damp cloth and wiped the blotches of wine away. Her skin was stained in places. She hadn't uttered a word throughout it all.

He looked up then, and it was as if a fist had slammed into his chest. She was crying, great silent tears that ran down her cheeks and dripped from her chin.

The old nice-guy Eric would have produced a clean handkerchief and petted her. Savage Eric merely looked away. "I think your skirt is ruined." He put an arm around her waist and lifted her long enough to strip the splotched fabric down her hips and tug it free.

He tossed the garment in the sink and bent to scoop up the shards of glass. Then he sprayed cleaner and wiped up the last of the mess. He was aware of her watching him. When he was finished, he rinsed off his hands and dried them with a dish towel.

He steeled himself to look at her. She sat perched like a sprite on the stool, her knees tucked to her chest, her arms tightly wound

around them. And she was nude from the waist down except for a pair of bright yellow bikini panties.

He swallowed hard. "Why are you crying?" he said gruffly.

Still she didn't acknowledge or try to halt the tears. "I don't know," she whispered. "You're so angry."

His lips twisted. "Did you think you had the corner on that emotion? I'm tired of apologizing, Shelby. Damned tired."

He leaned back against the counter, his hands braced behind him. Her face was tragic, totally devoid of the bright joy and humor he'd fallen in love with. Had he lost that woman forever?

The shaft of terror and dread that accompanied the thought scared the crap out of him, and the fear made him angrier still.

He saw the muscles in her throat work as she swallowed. She glanced at the clock. "The roast should be done by now."

Her deliberately prosaic statement ripped the fragile hold he had on his emotions. With one savage motion he flicked off the oven. "You should have asked me if I was hungry," he said, his tone just shy of insolent.

Her eyes widened. "You're always hungry."

He grunted. "Not lately. Other urges seem to have taken over. A man can only concentrate on one thing at a time."

She lifted her chin. "And what might that one thing be?" Even tearstained, she managed to look down her nose at him.

The chain holding back the beast snapped. "This," he said between clenched teeth. And he scooped her over his shoulder and headed for the hallway.

He made it only halfway up the stairs. His hand on her almost bare butt was telegraphing lewd messages to his brain. He stopped dead, his chest heaving, and set her on her feet. With barely leashed violence, he peeled her top up over her head, moaning aloud when he realized she wasn't wearing a bra. She was two steps above him, and her chest was at eye level.

He cupped her tits one at a time and sucked each nipple deep into his mouth. She had beautiful breasts, just large enough to fill a man's hands to overflowing. He squeezed them and stroked them and played with them, drunk with the pleasure of touching his wife.

He took her head in his hands and kissed her roughly, feeling dizzy and weak in the knees. He wasn't going to make it to the bed. That much was clear.

He reached down and ripped the narrow waistband of her panties. Too impatient to help her step out of them, he ripped the other side as well.

He gripped her hips and buried his face against her pussy, inhaling deeply. Dear God, how could he have gone so long without this? He tongued her deliberately and heard her soft cry. He thrust inside her tight passage with two fingers. She was hot and wet and swollen . . . as though she had already had sex today.

He jerked and went still, caught in the violent grip of devastating jealousy. Surely she hadn't . . . No. He knew Shelby better than that.

With a great shuddering breath, he went back to licking her,

loving the familiar taste, the seductive scent. She trembled in his grasp. He turned her around and forced her onto her knees, sprawled awkwardly over three steps.

With clumsy haste, he unzipped his pants and freed his cock. It was so hard, he hurt. It was too late to worry about whether his wife had forgiven him. He thought he might literally die if he didn't get inside her in the next thirty seconds.

He spread her legs and shoved deep in one desperate motion, burying himself balls-deep and staying there for one long, shuddering moment. The feel of her inner muscles squeezing him tightly made bright spots dance in front of his eyes.

He gasped for air, for reason. But it was a lost cause. He held on to her ass, his fingers digging into her pliant flesh. "Damn you, Shelby. Ten weeks and five days. Never again, goddammit. I can't live without you. Without this."

He knew he was taking her like a wild man, and he didn't care. Her pretty breasts were mashed against the berber carpet. Her bottom tipped toward him. He slid in and out quickly, trying to hold back the inevitable. He reached beneath her and lightly stroked her clit. Shelby climaxed with a small cry, and her capitulation sent him over the edge.

He fucked her hard, again and again, pistoning strokes that ended abruptly when hot fire gripped his sex and exploded in an endless ejaculation. He was almost sobbing as the last spasm wrenched him.

He pulled out and changed their positions, tugging Shelby

onto his lap as he sat. His cock was still hard, perhaps not the iron rod it had been moments ago, but still more than capable of getting the job done.

Shelby seemed dazed, her pupils dilated, her mouth slack. He lifted her and impaled her on his cock, then took both her arms behind her back and held her wrists with his left hand.

With his free hand he pinched her nipples. "Ride me, Shelby."

She moved with sinuous grace, her head thrown back, her blond hair a messy tangle. She whimpered when he pulled roughly at her nipples. Both were hard and distended, deep raspberry pink.

He raked them with his teeth, inhaling the perfume she had applied in her cleavage. He had a sudden flash of another man's hand touching his wife, but he doggedly pushed it away.

She began to get tired, so he leaned back and thrust upward, going deeper still at this angle. He released her arms. "Hold my neck," he demanded.

She obeyed, and he buried his face in her breasts, his arms going around her waist. He wanted to make this moment last forever. Being so close to her was healing the raw places in his soul. He wanted to be so deep inside her they could never separate.

Amazingly, given his recent explosive climax, he still wasn't able to make this round last much longer than the first. He groaned in dismay as he felt his release bearing down. Shelby was limp in his arms, her breathing labored. He bit her neck. "I'm coming, honey. Oh, God, too damned soon."

Raw sensation ripped him, turned him inside out. He groaned and jerked and shuddered as he came, vaguely aware in some peripheral corner of his mind that Shelby had joined him in the final moments.

And then, with tears burning the backs of his eyelids, he crushed her close and held her in silence, too weary to do more than pray in random incoherent phrases that his wife wanted him back.

Chapter Four

Shelby rested her head against Eric's shoulder and tried to catch her breath. He had never made love to her like that before. Ever. Eric was a gentleman in the bedroom. A sensual, generous, multitalented gentleman, but a gentleman nevertheless.

The man who held her now was a rough-edged, dominant wolf. The transformation was both disconcerting and arousing. She wasn't quite sure how to respond.

She stroked his hair with soft, tender touches. She loved him desperately. And she had missed their lovemaking every bit as much as he had.

There were things that needed to be said, but the night was

young. She sat up, raking her hair from her face. Despite the seriousness of their situation, it amused her that Eric had trouble dragging his gaze from her breasts to her face.

She managed a smile. "*Now* are you hungry?"

His sheepish expression tugged at her heart. He looked guilty and adorably uncertain. He stood up, managing to scoop her into his arms and pull up his pants at the same time. He dropped his forehead to hers. "We need to clean up first."

He carried her to the bedroom and deposited her gently on her feet before disappearing into the bathroom. While Eric filled their hot tub, she brushed her hair and hunted out some new clothes. When the water was ready, steaming hot and scented with her favorite frangipani bath salts, he held out a hand. "Ladies first."

It took all the poise she could muster to twine her fingers with his and allow him to help her into the tub. It had been weeks since either of them had been naked in front of the other. He had undressed while she was in the bedroom, and the sight of his virile, masculine body made her weak in the knees.

When she was settled, he scooted in beside her, sloshing water over the edge as he got seated. He leaned his head back with a sigh. "Feels good," he said quietly, his words slightly slurred.

He had dark circles beneath his eyes, and his shoulders slumped with exhaustion. No wonder. Even as she had been saying good-bye to Jason, she'd been aware of Eric's car parked nearby. He had been her protector last night, barely beating her into bed sometime before four. And although she had been able to sleep late, he'd had to be up at the normal time getting ready for work.

Her heart ached for what must have gone through his mind while he sat and waited for her last night. For her part, knowing Eric had screwed another woman hurt like nothing she had ever felt before. But how much worse would it have been if she'd been sitting just outside the door while he did it?

She clenched her hands together beneath the water and took a big breath. "Eric. I forgave you a long time ago. Honestly. I was just having trouble letting go of the anger. I'm sorry."

He blinked once and his eyes focused, his mouth a grim line. "Thank you. I don't deserve your forgiveness, but I swear you'll never have cause to doubt me again."

His humility embarrassed her. "Let's be honest, Eric. We both know it was as much my fault as yours. I've beat you up over this, but part of the reason I was so upset was because I was ashamed. I failed you as a wife. And I don't even know why I was so stupid. You mean everything to me, Eric...." Her words trailed off as her throat tightened and clogged with emotion.

He glided across the small space that separated them and wrapped his arms around her. "I'm proud of the work you do, honey. You're smart and full of energy and enthusiasm. You just got a little carried away, that's all."

The gentle teasing in his voice made her tears fall in earnest.

He held her while she sobbed away two months of grief and anguish. This whole fiasco had been the first real test of their marriage, and she couldn't believe it was over.

Resting against his broad, strong chest and feeling the steady strength of his love made her realize how scared she had been. Scared that the bond between them had been irreparably damaged. But the tender kisses he pressed along her hairline and at her ear and throat spoke more loudly than words of the depths of his love, in spite of everything. Her heart ached with relief.

It was too soon for happiness. That emotion would have to wait. For now, she could concentrate on nothing but a profound gratitude that she and Eric had weathered this storm. And she made a vow to watch over her husband and her marriage much more carefully.

When her tears had dwindled to sniffles, he used his fingertips to wipe her cheeks. His dark eyes glowed with joy, and the emotion in them made her want to weep all over again.

He smiled a lopsided grin. "I'd offer you a handkerchief, but I seem to be a bit underdressed at the moment."

She laughed softly. "I'm not complaining." She screwed up her courage. "About last night . . ."

For a brief moment misery flashed through his eyes, but he regained his smile with an obvious effort. "Not now," he said, his voice thick and unsteady. "It will keep."

She hesitated. She had a confession to make, and she wanted to start over with a clean slate. But the rigid set of his jaw warned her that now might not be the best time to unburden her conscience.

So she swallowed her misgivings and returned his smile with one of her own. "Then let's go eat," she said, speaking with deliberate lightness. "I'm starving."

She dressed in clean clothes similar to what she had worn earlier, but minus the pretty panties. No point in ruining a second pair. And she was pretty sure that Eric had plans for the rest of the evening.

With a little help from the microwave, the meal was salvageable. Eric ate with enthusiasm, and although she was nervous about the night to come, she forced enough food down that he wasn't suspicious.

At one point in the evening she almost abandoned her plan to spill her guts. Doing so might shatter their fragile accord. After all, why was it necessary? She had seduced another man with Eric's knowledge and consent. Did it matter what she had felt with Bar Guy between her legs? What she learned? How she climaxed?

Eric asked her a question, and she forced her attention back to the present, shuddering inwardly as the memories made her weak. What kind of woman was she? She had reconciled with her husband, and she couldn't stop thinking about a tawdry night of cheap sex.

When they finished eating, they cleaned up the kitchen in amicable harmony, speaking seldom, but pausing occasionally to share a kiss.

Shelby had set the table with her great-grandmother's china and silver, so they didn't use the dishwasher. Eric washed each piece with care, and she dried them and returned them to the china cabinet.

When the kitchen and dining room were spotless, Eric folded the dishcloth neatly over the edge of the sink and looked at her inquiringly. "Do you feel like watching a movie? We haven't seen all of that new DVD set you bought last week."

She debated for a moment, nibbling her bottom lip. It wasn't late. Plenty of time for a movie. But she wanted her husband again, and before that could happen, she had to tell him the truth.

She sighed. "Eric . . . we need to talk about last night."

He winced and squeezed his eyes shut. "I followed you last night," he muttered. "I know more or less what happened. I was there for most of it." Guilt shadowed his face, and any joy from their earlier conversation had disappeared completely.

"I know," she said softly. "And I was glad. You made me feel safe, and I needed that."

Some of the torment in his eyes lifted, and he smiled faintly. "I couldn't let you go off alone, honey. Too many crazies in the world. But I wasn't spying on you, I swear."

She nodded. She should have started this conversation while they were still working. Now there was nothing to do with her hands. She linked them behind her back, licking her lips nervously. "I'd like tell you about it, Eric. And then we never have to talk about it again."

He was staring at the floor, his head bowed.

When he didn't answer, she took his hand and led him upstairs.

As they crossed the threshold into their bedroom, Eric groaned and pulled her into his arms. His thick erection pressing against her belly shouldn't have surprised her. The man was a freaking Energizer Bunny tonight.

His arms were so tight, she finally protested.

He loosened his hold with a hoarse apology. And then he pulled away completely and shoved his hands in his pockets. "I have some ground rules," he said, not meeting her eyes.

Puzzlement made her tilt her head. "About?"

"This conversation."

She wrinkled her nose, seriously confused. "I'm not sure I understand."

He hissed out a frustrated breath. "Apparently you need to tell me some things, and I suppose I need to hear them, but we'll do this my way or not at all."

"Okay," she said slowly, not sure where this was going.

He started stripping off his clothes while she watched in amazement. "What in the heck are you doing?"

He faced her, his eyes hooded, a dark flush of color staining each cheekbone. "I want you to tie me to the bed. When you've finished doing that, you're not to touch me at all . . . while you're talking."

He was nude now. He threw back the covers on their king-size

bed and sprawled on his back. He looked fierce and very un-happy. His penis was flaccid.

She rummaged in a drawer for a couple of scarves. Then she went to the closet and retrieved two of his older ties. His eyes were closed, so she moved around the bed, carefully tying each of his long, muscular limbs firmly to a bedpost, checking each knot to make sure he couldn't pull free.

She wasn't immune to the provocative task. Hot shivers of arousal flickered in her womb.

When she was done, she curled up in the armchair beside the bed. Eric's face was a mask of tension, his eyes still tightly closed.

She drummed her fingers on the arms of the chair. "Now?"

He nodded, a quick jerk of his head that could have signaled assent or protest.

She sighed. "You saw that I went to a bar." It was a question of sorts, but Eric didn't move.

She continued. "Basically, I asked the bartender if he was in-terested in having sex with me. It was all pretty intimidating, if you want to know the truth. Propositioning him, deciding where to go. Actually checking in. My heart was in my throat the entire time. I really wanted to throw up."

She paused a moment, reliving the mix of dread and arousal. She wouldn't mention the arousal just yet. "Once we were in the room, we exchanged first names. We both took quick showers.

When he came out, he was wearing one of those thin motel towels and nothing else. He was . . ." She stopped and cleared her throat. "Erect."

She paused and stared at her husband bound in their bed, but his face was blank. She shifted in the chair, rubbing herself surreptitiously. Moisture already seeped between her legs. Talking about last night to Eric was affecting her in surprising ways.

She wished suddenly that she had brought up a bottle of water. She closed her eyes and leaned her head back in the chair. She couldn't look at him for the rest. "We kissed. . . ." A muffled groan from the bed startled her, but she continued. "It was . . . nice. Different, but nice. Then he got . . . Well, we both . . . I mean . . ."

"You both got hot." Eric's voice was flat.

"Yes," she whispered. "He took me down to the bed and I felt his penis pushing—"

"His cock. Say it, Shelby."

She frowned, seeing it all again like a movie behind her eyelids. "Okay, his cock, Eric. His cock was pushing inside me, and we started to make . . . we started having sex."

She paused, shaking all over. Repeating this out loud and keeping the explanation clinical and unemotional was no walk in the park. Each word she spoke meant reliving the night before.

"Go on."

She chanced one quick peek and then closed her eyes again. Eric's hands were fisted against the ties that held him immobile.

His entire body looked as though he were stretched painfully on a rack. But she knew for a fact that she had left a comfortable amount of slack in his restraints.

"Afterward I told him he could leave. He refused. We cleaned up some and then he sat on my chest and he was hard again. But we didn't have another condom. So he jerked off on my breasts."

She actually heard the great shudder that racked Eric's body as he muttered a string of curses beneath his breath.

Doggedly, she went on. "Then he ate me until I had an orgasm, and I think we slept for a little bit. Then I came home."

She fell silent, exhausted by the effort of keeping all emotion from her voice. Her heart was racing and her mouth was dry.

She refused to look at him as the silence grew and lengthened.

His voice was ragged when he finally spoke. "Look at me, Shelby."

She obeyed, and sucked in a shocked breath. His eyes glittered with shards of heat. His chest rose and fell with labored breathing. And he had an erection. A heavy, straining, huge erection.

His lips twisted in self-derision. "I wanted you to see me like this, Shelby. So I couldn't hide my reactions. Last night while you were seducing some random guy, I was getting hard. Just like now. So maybe I'm more of a jerk than you thought, and maybe you want to think twice before you forgive me."

She saw his throat work, and he continued. "I hated what was happening. I wanted to drag the guy outside and beat him to a pulp, but God help me, Shelby . . . some strange bastard put his prick in your cunt and I got off on it. You must think I'm a—"

She sprang to her feet. "Shut up." She practically screamed it.

His mouth fell open, and the self-loathing on his face morphed into pained confusion.

She clenched her hands at her hips. "Enough of your noble confessions, Eric. I'm the one in trouble here." Her voice trembled, and her breath came in short, sharp pants.

She shrugged unhappily. "As soon as it was over, I wanted to do it again." *So there.* She didn't actually say the last two words out loud, but she might as well have. He got the message.

She saw shock and anger and something indecipherable flash across his face.

"See, Eric," she said wearily. "I think I was lying to both of us about evening the score. I think I used your infidelity as an excuse to satisfy my curiosity about being with another man. So who's the bastard now? Or I guess *bitch* would be the more proper term."

She sank to her knees beside the bed and buried her face in her hands. She couldn't bear to look at him. All these months he'd worn the hair shirt of repentance, and his two-faced wife wanted her own walk on the wild side.

She didn't know what to do. Where did they go from here?

It might have been minutes or hours before his harsh voice broke the silence. "Go get him."

Her head jerked up. "What?"

His features were carved in stone, only his eyes alive. And his

cock was still at attention. "Bring him here so he can have you again. But this time I won't be shut out."

"Are you out of your mind?" she whispered, but his quiet command had liquefied her bones. Everything inside her melted. Her breasts swelled. Her sex tingled and throbbed.

"What if he's not there? What if he won't come?"

"He'll come."

She stood and leaned to untie one of his arms.

"No." His abrupt command stilled her movement. "This will be my punishment."

"That's crazy," she cried. "What if the house catches on fire? What if you have to go to the bathroom? What if you—"

"Go, Shelby. And hurry."

She spared him one last incredulous glance. His penis reared proud and long against his belly. The muscles in his arms and chest gleamed with sweat, although the room was not particularly warm.

But it was his eyes that touched her the most. The swirl of emotions in his steady gaze captured arousal, chagrin, hope, and maybe a touch of dread.

She touched his ankle. "I'll be back as soon as I can."

She drove like a madwoman, pausing at intersections only to avoid getting a ticket or causing an accident. Her hands on the wheel were slick with perspiration. Her stomach felt queasy. Eric was willing for her to have one more naughty fling . . . as long as he could watch. *Sweet Jesus.*

The university was ten minutes away. She made it in eight. She parallel-parked a shade too close to a fire hydrant and jumped out of the car.

When she walked though the door and saw him at the bar, her heart crashed into her belly. Relief. Shocked disbelief. Anxiety.

She rushed toward him, skidding to a stop and hopping onto a bar stool. It took him ninety seconds to finish serving a customer and head her way. She counted.

The flash of pleasure on his face calmed her some. He gave her a crooked grin. "Hey, Shelby with no last name."

She grabbed his hand. "I need you to come home with me."

The smile faded and his eyes narrowed. "You in trouble with the big guy? And I'm supposed to reassure him that nothing happened?"

She drew back, shocked for some reason. "Of course not." Then she leaned forward again, lowering her voice. "I told him I wanted to have . . ." She looked around uneasily.

His rough whisper was barely audible. "Sex with me?"

She nodded jerkily. "He agreed. But you have to come with me now."

For another thirty seconds he studied her face. Lord knew what he saw there. He pulled his cell phone from his pocket and dialed a number, conversing softly with whoever answered. Finally the phone flipped shut. "Okay."

She hissed. "Okay what?"

"My buddy's going to cover the rest of my shift."

"How soon can he be here?"

He shrugged. "Twenty, thirty minutes, depending on traffic. What's the rush?"

Her stomach clenched as she remembered Eric helpless and alone. "Can the manager cover until your friend gets here? Tell him it's an emergency."

He shook his head and sighed. "I'll see. But if this is supposed to be an emergency, you'd better wait where no one can see you."

He disappeared through a door in the back, and she fled from the bar. She hovered just outside, peering through the window until she saw Jason heading her way. When he stepped out onto the sidewalk, she touched his arm. "Can you follow me in your car?"

He just shook his head. "Sure. For you, Shelby, anything."

To his credit he kept up with her kamikaze driving. When they pulled up in her driveway and she looked at her watch, she estimated Eric had been alone for almost forty minutes.

They entered the house in silence. She saw Jason look around with interest, but her thoughts were on her husband. In the upstairs hallway she indicated the open door of a guest room. "Do you mind sitting in here for a few minutes? I need to let him know we're home."

She didn't wait to see Jason's reaction. She slipped quietly into the master bedroom and locked the door behind her.

Eric's eyes were closed when she first walked in, but they flew open instantly. "Did he come?"

Her lips trembled. "Yes."

His grin was wry. "Told you he would."

She untied each of the knots, and Eric gathered her into his arms. He held her tightly. "You sure about this?"

She nodded slowly. "What will *you* do?"

His chest heaved once in a deep sigh. "Sit in the chair."

"And if he protests?"

The implacable wolf was back. "Then no deal."

Their lips met, his hot and hungry, hers clinging with sudden panic. Her legs had lost all their strength, and she leaned into Eric, desperately trying to soak up his quiet confidence.

She stroked the muscular planes of his back, drunk with the knowledge that she could touch him again. So long, so damned long since they had shared this precious intimacy.

He slapped her on the butt. "Quit stalling. Give me five minutes and come back."

He grabbed a pair of jeans and a T-shirt from the drawer and disappeared into the bathroom.

She quietly unlocked the door and stepped out into the hall. It was only a matter of five or six steps to the room where Jason sat waiting, but it felt like miles. Her hands were icy cold.

He was sprawled in a small vanity chair, his careless masculine grace dwarfing the small seat. He lifted an eyebrow. "I thought you'd forgotten me."

She shook her head. "No." Her throat dried up and she couldn't think of a single word to say.

Jason stood and took her in his arms. He kissed her gently. "I don't think I'm up for anything kinky, pretty Shelby. I don't do guy on guy, even for a lark."

She played with the hair at the back of his neck. "That's not what this is about. I want to have sex with you again. That's all."

"And the hubby?"

"He'll be in there."

"He wants to watch?"

"Yes."

"What if I can't perform under those conditions?"

His tone was teasing, but she wondered if he was half-serious. She cupped his balls, squeezed lightly, and heard him groan. "I don't think it will be a problem. Just concentrate on me."

She took him by the hand and led him toward her bedroom. The door was ajar. The room was shadowy, illuminated only by the light from the bathroom and one small candle burning on her bedside table.

Eric sat in the same chair she had occupied earlier. He was barefooted. One leg was slung over the arm of the chair and the other foot rested on the floor. Despite his seemingly relaxed posture, she could see tension in the deliberate stillness of his body.

She hesitated in the doorway, paralyzed by shyness.

Eric crooked his finger. "Come on in, Shelby."

Jason released her hand and followed her in silence. The two men sized each other up, their silent, edgy, testosterone-laden challenge just below the surface.

Both men were equally attractive. Both men shared a quiet confidence. She shivered as heat slithered down her spine and settled low in her belly. Her breasts tightened in anticipation.

Eric spoke quietly. "Pretend I'm not here."

Jason's gaze skittered from Eric to the empty bed and back to Shelby's face. She saw and heard him suck in a raw breath. "Okay, then," he mumbled.

Jason took both of her hands in his. She was pretty sure the tremors in their clasped fingers weren't coming only from her.

She felt as though everything in her body were frozen. She could see. She could hear. She could feel. God, could she feel. But she didn't know what to do next. She knew what arousal felt like. Recognized the hot bite of pleasure, the knife edge of anticipation. But the honeyed urgency curling like a seductive serpent in her sex scared her to death.

Jason lifted her hands one at a time to his lips and kissed her knuckles, his tongue raking across bone and flesh, causing her knees to buckle.

He caught her around the waist, bringing her flush against his hips. His thick, heavy erection pressed into her stomach. He kissed her ear and the tender skin beneath. His hot whisper ruffled the curls at her neck. "It's showtime, honey. Don't be afraid."

And then his mouth found hers and her whole world began to spin out of control.

There was nothing tentative about the kiss. Hunger and the

piquant bite of the forbidden fueled the fire. Jason was more forceful than he had been the night before, perhaps because her body was no longer unfamiliar to him, but more likely because he was aware of their audience of one.

She shivered in his grasp, feeling his urgency. He scooped her up and deposited her on the bed, following her down and ripping at her clothes. He found her bare ass and cursed softly, his hands squeezing and kneading her flesh. She helped him remove her top and skirt and then they went to work on his clothes.

The seconds until they were both naked seemed like an eternity. She reached for his cock, but he stilled her hand with a hoarse protest. "Not yet."

He lifted himself on an elbow and looked down at her. His eyes were hooded, his lips pressed together in a straight line. She lay perfectly still as his large palm skated from her shoulder to her breasts, hovered there for a moment, and then slid down her belly to her pussy.

For a split second, her eyes darted to Eric, and she tried to gauge his reaction. But his face was in shadow, and she couldn't even see his eyes.

Jason slid a finger deep inside her pussy, rotating his thumb over her clit at the same time. She whimpered as hot tendrils of flame burst and spread. Unconsciously, her right hand reached out to Eric. She needed something to hold on to, a familiar anchor in this almost frightening journey. But there was nothing there.

She felt the press of Jason's cock at her hip. Her breathing quickened. Conscious thought slipped away, shoved aside by pleasure, dark and deep.

A groan struggled from deep inside her chest as a powerful climax bore down on her. Jason bent and nipped her breast, sucking hard at a nipple. She screamed. Her world went black. And she tumbled and fell until all she could feel were tidal-force ripples in her pussy, squeezing and contracting over and over until the last sparkling jolt faded into mist.

Chapter Five

Eric realized he had never fully appreciated his wife's orgasms until that moment. It was a painful perspective, but enlightening. Shelby's fair skin was flushed and damp, her hair tumbled across the pillow in disarray. Her nipples were hard as pebbles, her breasts pink and inviting.

Her soft, full lips were parted, and the raw sexual sounds she made were the most arousing things he had ever heard. When her hand reached in his direction, he had to grip the arms of the chair to keep from going to her. Her eyes were squeezed shut, so she never saw his involuntary move in her direction.

But Bar Guy saw. No, wait . . . What did Shelby call him? Jason? Jason looked his way for a split second, distracted momentarily by Eric's unwitting movement. Their eyes met briefly, and Jason smiled. Eric wanted to wipe that smug, triumphant grin from the guy's face. He was here on sufferance—didn't he know that?

Jason lifted Shelby's thighs to his shoulders and buried his face between her legs. He licked and sucked greedily, tasting the cream of Shelby's climax.

Eric knew that flavor intimately, craved it like a drug. Blood pooled in his groin. His cock swelled and hardened, though he would have sworn he was already at maximum readiness.

He unzipped his jeans and freed himself, squeezing his prick and jerking his hand up and down on the shaft. He wanted desperately to relieve the gnawing ache, but he was afraid that in his release he would miss something happening on the bed.

So he kept himself on the knife-edge of arousal, playing with his cock and balls, but getting no enjoyment from it. Torture was a more apt description.

The couple's murmured conversation was barely audible. But he could hear the excitement in Shelby's breathless voice, the delight and arousal in her husky moans. She cried out sharply as she peaked again, and her hands fisted in Jason's hair, holding him close as she shuddered and quivered in a second climax.

Eric watched, stunned, as she rode out the orgasm. Jason never let up, his mouth driving her higher and higher. When Shelby went limp, Jason flopped beside her, pulling her into his arms.

Eric felt incredulous and inadequate. Had he ever given his

sensual wife such indisputable satisfaction? Were their sexual encounters as raw and unscripted? As carnal? As fulfilling?

The nasty seed of doubt filled his belly with bile, and his cock went limp. He felt the sting of defeated tears and blinked them back angrily. Damned if he would let Jason see him crumble.

He scrubbed a hand over his face and swallowed hard. This pain would be over soon, the razor-sharp scrape on his emotions just a memory. He wanted to leave, but he couldn't make his legs move. He didn't want to see any more.

But the worst of it was just getting started.

Shelby roused finally and kissed Jason with ardent gratitude and affection. Her face was an open book. No one could have missed the satisfaction in her sated expression.

She lay half across Jason's chest, and his arm that wasn't cradling her came up to cup her butt. She wriggled and shrieked when he slipped a hand between her legs and tickled her labia from behind.

Shelby scooted down on the bed and took Jason's cock in her mouth. Eric bit his lip until it nearly bled, stifling his instinctive outraged protest with dogged determination.

Seeing his wife's lips wrapped around strange meat was a knife to the heart. But his body overruled his brain. His cock rose again, stimulated against his will by the titillating picture.

Shelby cupped the guy's balls, pulling at them gently as she sucked hard at the head of his prick. Jason was writhing and groaning, his body taut with hunger.

Eric watched the erotic tableau, unable to look away even for a second. The two on the bed had long since forgotten his quiet presence.

Jason visibly neared the edge. He shoved Shelby away, grabbed his pants off the floor, and pulled out a handful of condoms, tossing all but one on the bedside table. He sheathed himself in a quick move and tumbled Shelby over onto her knees. He shoved pillows beneath her stomach, smashed her shoulders and face into the mattress, and spread her legs. With a loud, choked grunt, he buried himself from behind into her pussy.

Eric clutched at his own erection, trying vainly to appease the ache. Every thrust of Jason's cock reverberated in Eric's gut. He could almost feel Shelby's inner muscles gripping him. He used his thumb to spread the drop of moisture on the head of his cock. The lightest touch was agony.

He felt the unmistakable surge of his orgasm bearing down on him, and he squirmed in the chair. Not yet. God, not yet. He had to see Shelby. Her face was obscured by the fall of her hair. *Shit.* He needed to look at her. He was compelled to watch her pleasure.

Jason withdrew suddenly, wringing a muffled cry of protest from the woman in the subservient position. Jason moved her roughly, as though he were handling a rag doll. He positioned

himself so that his back was against the headboard and impaled Shelby on his cock, facing away from him.

Now Eric had an unobstructed view. Was that Jason's intent? His way of taunting Eric?

Jason pulled Shelby's arms behind her back and secured her wrists in one of his big hands. With the other hand he reached around and teased her breasts, plucking and pulling at her nipples while he thrust upward with pistonlike force.

Shelby quickly caught his rhythm. She put her feet flat on the bed beside his hips, and her mouth flew open in a shocked, silent scream when the new angle enabled Jason to go even deeper into her cunt.

Jason abandoned her tits and touched her where their bodies joined. Eric saw him tease her clit. Shelby's head was thrown back on Jason's shoulder, her cheek pressed against his chin. She turned and kissed him, and Jason froze for a moment, his mouth dueling with hers in a desperate dance.

Shelby's back arched, making her beautiful breasts rise. She was panting, her eyes closed, the muscles in her arms straining against Jason's hold.

Eric watched the incandescent passion on his wife's face with dull despair. She was like a mythical creature, totally lost in hedonistic pleasure, completely abandoned in her quest for fulfillment. Her shining beauty blinded him.

Jason bit her neck, pumping harder. Shelby cried out and

crested the peak. Jason released her arms and gripped her hips as he unloaded his come in spasm after spasm of climax.

When it was all over, the silence in the room was broken only by the sound of three sets of ragged breathing, each harsh, uneven sigh a mute commentary on what was too powerful for words.

When Shelby and Jason seemed to drift into sleep, Eric rose to his feet like an old man. He hobbled across the room silently, his bare feet making no sound at all in the lush, thick carpet.

He went to the guest room across the hall and shut the door. In the bathroom mirror he examined his face. The pallor, the skin stretched tight over angular cheekbones. The dark torment in his eyes.

But then the image in the mirror faded. He saw his wife's wide eyes, her rosy lips, her ivory skin. He saw the tip of her tongue wet her lips as her eyelids fluttered closed. He saw a man's long fingers tease his wife's nipples. Saw a man's long, thick penis slide between his wife's thighs and impale her.

And then, as he saw his lovely wife's expression reflect the intense, fiery pleasure gripping her body, his hand moved faster and faster on his cock and he came with a muffled shout, splattering come into the sink and against the wall, and then collapsing to his knees with a moan of surrender.

Shelby sighed and stretched, feeling the unmistakable effects of sexual excess. Jason lay beside her, snoring softly.

She turned her head and looked at the chair. It was empty. A slither of unease tightened her stomach, and then she relaxed. Eric was probably in the bathroom. Or maybe he had gone for a drink.

She glanced at the clock. She and Jason had been at it for almost an hour. She was desperate to know how Eric had reacted. It had been so awkward in the beginning. She had been painfully conscious of Eric's watchful gaze as Jason touched and kissed her.

But at some point the physical sensations had overtaken her mental hesitation. Her young body had wrested control from her overanalytical mind, and she had immersed herself wholeheartedly in the enjoyment of the moment.

Jason was good in bed. But certainly no better than Eric. Nothing Jason had initiated was shocking or different. It was the knowledge that her husband watched as another man pleasured her that made her crazy. In a good way. Her arousal was stronger and quicker, her orgasms more intense. She had practically wallowed in sex, and it felt damned good.

A hand tickled her belly, signaling Jason's wakefulness. She smiled at him. He smiled back. Their shared intimacy made friendship seem like a possibility, though her rational mind rejected that prospect instantly.

Jason nudged her with his erection.

Her eyebrows went up. "Again?"

His smile was lopsided. "What can I say? You inspire me."

He tried to move between her legs, but she stopped him.

"I don't think so, Jason. Eric left, and I don't know where he is. I need to check on him."

Jason fondled her breasts and grazed her clitoris with a featherlight touch. "He's a big boy," he muttered, kissing his way down her cleavage. "And besides . . . I'm pretty damn sure I'll never see you again after tonight, so please, pretty Shelby with no last name, let me fuck you one last time."

He didn't wait for verbal permission, taking the instinctive spread of her legs as all the assent needed. This time he entered her with exquisite slowness. She was supersensitive, even a little bit sore, and the press of his thick cock against her swollen flesh was almost too much stimulation.

She should have protested more strongly, but she was pretty sure Jason was right. She couldn't imagine Eric tolerating his wife's extracurricular activities beyond this one strange night.

Jason moved and she gasped. Besides . . . her appetite for sex had not been fully appeased. She knew her plans to seduce Eric as soon as Jason was gone were sound, but in the meantime, arousal still hummed like an insistent tune in her veins.

She wanted this one last screw.

Across the hall, sprawled on the bed, Eric heard them start up again, and he wanted to howl with rage and protest. God, were they going to fuck all night? In his bed?

He pulled a pillow over his head and pressed it against his ears. When that didn't work, he flipped the clock radio to FM

and listened to a stock market report. The one time he silenced the radio and dared to sit up and listen, he heard more than he bargained for.

Grimly, he tossed the pillow aside and got to his feet. Three could play this particular game, and if the other two didn't like it, well . . . that was just too damned bad.

Seeing Eric appear in the doorway shocked Shelby into a sudden orgasm. She'd been thinking about him watching . . . while Jason moved between her legs. This climax was sweeter, less intense. She was getting tired. She was pretty sure Jason hadn't realized yet that their audience was back.

When he surged inside her one last time and groaned, she held his hips. Still Eric watched. Still he didn't move.

She waited, panting, until Jason rolled onto his back. Her eyes met her husband's, hers questioning, his darkly intense.

Eric moved into the room toward the bed. His posture suggested a beast on the prowl. A man with a mission. Any cliché you might choose to describe single-minded, implacable determination. His resolute demeanor sent shivers down her spine. Amazingly, she felt the first tingles of renewed arousal.

Jason's eyes were closed, but they flew open when Eric's approach made a soft sound on the carpet. Jason scrambled to a sitting position with the sheet clutched to his chest. A brief look of panic crossed his face, and then sheer, masculine bravado replaced it.

Shelby understood his unease and his need to cover the family jewels. Eric looked capable of castrating him. Fortunately, Shelby lay between the two bristling males. She held out a hand to her scowling husband. "Are you joining us?"

A reluctant smile creased his cheeks for a moment. "Is that an invitation?"

She nibbled her bottom lip, realizing in a flash that her night was about to get far more interesting. "I wasn't aware you needed one. This is your bed."

Eric smirked. "Yeah. It is." He glared at Jason as he said it.

Jason was pretty cool, under the circumstances. He managed to look bored and confident at the same time. She had to give him snaps for that. Eric in a temper was pretty menacing.

She sucked in a breath when Eric began stripping off his clothes. Beside her, Jason moved uneasily. She sat up herself and scrambled for some way to defuse the situation. Beneath the sheet she patted Jason's hand. "Maybe you should go now," she whispered.

Eric's face darkened. "He stays." He said it with blunt arrogance, clearly defying either of them to complain.

Jason's fingers, still hidden, squeezed hers. He lifted his chin. "In the chair or in the bed?"

Eric hesitated for a split second, his cock flexing hungrily as it reared against his abdomen. He frowned. "I guess that's up to Shelby."

Her stomach knotted. *Oh, shit.* She wasn't prepared to make

this decision. What should she say? Would Eric be pissed if she allowed Jason to remain for the next act? Would Jason be too intimidated to enjoy it?

She swallowed hard. "In the bed," she muttered. She was pretty sure she heard both men groan in unison.

In one smooth, forceful motion, Eric ripped the sheet to the foot of the bed. Ignoring Jason, he came down beside Shelby and took her in his arms. His mouth zeroed in on hers, kissing her with rough, hungry yearning. His erection pressed urgently against her hip.

She twined her arms around his neck. He felt so wonderfully warm and familiar. She arched her back and parted her legs, trying to urge him on.

He didn't take the hint. He moved to her breast, sucking so hard she gasped. A spear of hot arousal shifted through her, leaving her breathless. Again she tried to move him between her legs.

But Eric had other plans. He lifted his head to stare at Jason. He was breathing hard, and his cheeks were flushed. "Move up there and hold her hands."

It took Jason only a second to get the idea. While Eric dragged Shelby lower in the bed, Jason sat against the headboard and grabbed her hands, stretching her arms and holding them firmly.

She cried out, feeling everything between her legs quiver with heat and become drenched with moisture. Her head rested against Jason's thigh.

Eric spread her legs wide, stretching the muscles in her thighs almost unbearably. Suddenly she was subdued, helpless, at the mercy of two men. Her heart was pounding so hard she was having trouble catching her breath. She was trembling and weak, racked with shivers, alternately hot and cold.

Aside from that one terse command, Eric ignored Jason. Her husband stared at her pussy as if he had never seen one before. His eyes were hooded, his features sharp. He bent his head and blew on her clitoris.

She flinched, even though it was nothing more than a brush of warm air. Her arms tugged instinctively to be free. But Jason's hold was unbreakable.

Eric crouched farther and licked her with one deliberate pass of his tongue. She jerked and cried out. His hands were braced just below her knees, keeping her legs apart.

She was already hovering on the precipice of a blinding climax. And unfortunately, her husband knew her body so well, he was able to gauge exactly how much stimulation she could bear without tumbling into the abyss. And so the torture began.

He tongued the sensitive skin of her inner thighs. He left little love bites in the soft white flesh near the top of her legs. He teased her belly button and wet the fluff of curls below with his tongue.

And then suddenly, he lifted his head and acknowledged the other man with a steady gaze. She couldn't see Jason's expression, but some message passed between the two. Eric returned

to his lazy caresses, and Jason shifted both of her wrists to one of his big hands.

Even so, his grip was inescapable. With his newly freed hand, he got into mischief.

She shrieked when Jason pinched her nipple at the exact moment Eric nibbled her clit. She would have come right then, but her diabolical captors left her just shy of the prize.

They changed their attack to her arms. Jason stroked her neck and collarbone while Eric licked the sensitive skin from her armpit up to her elbow.

She tried to evade his touch. "That tickles," she panted.

Eric sucked a nipple into his mouth. Jason played with the whorl of her ear. Her entire body was taut with longing. She made incoherent, pleading murmurs, begging for mercy.

The two men were silent, intent with an odd sort of unspoken collusion on driving her completely out of her mind.

Eric finally abandoned her aching breasts and moved back down in the bed, this time far too low for her liking. He began kissing her feet, sucking at the tender arches and licking her anklebones.

Jason teased her damp nipples, circling them with his fingernail and every now and then tugging and pulling at the tight peaks until she moaned. Every inch of her body ached with a hunger that raced through her bloodstream and settled in her bones.

Finally, when she was almost incoherent with an arousal unlike anything she had ever before experienced, Eric moved between her legs. He lifted her thighs and cupped her butt. The blunt head of his cock teased but didn't enter.

He wasn't even looking at her. He was looking at Jason. "Kiss her," he said, in a voice that brooked no opposition.

Jason moved awkwardly, still keeping her arms immobile, but settling beside her. His mouth found hers, and she felt the insistent press of his tongue just as Eric probed and then shoved deep.

She shattered into a million pieces. Invaded simultaneously by a demanding tongue and a surging cock, held immobile as her body accepted two men, she arched into a climax that jerked her to the top of a mountain and then flung her, sobbing and shivering, into space.

When she regained her senses, Eric lay sprawled beside her, his chest rising and falling in a deep sleep. Jason was stroking her breast with tender, easy touches. His erection pressed against her hip.

She saw the hunger on his face. The need. The pained uncertainty.

She smiled at him. "Yes."

It was all the encouragement he needed. He tugged her to the soft carpet, eager and sure, and entered her carefully. She appreciated his gentleness. She was sore and well-used. But she couldn't deny him this one last moment.

He rode her steadily to his brief, intense orgasm. She stroked his back, feeling emotions she couldn't even name. Afterward, he slid from her body and stood. He looked down at her with a wry smile. "Time for me to go, I think."

He disappeared into the bathroom and then reappeared and got dressed rapidly.

It was almost one in the morning when she escorted him to his car. It was chilly outside, and she wrapped her red silk robe tightly around her and tied the sash. Jason looked rumpled and tired, but the lines of his face were softened by satisfaction.

She touched his arm. "Thank you."

He shrugged, his expression guarded despite the intimacies they had shared. "I think I should be thanking you," he said quietly. "You're pretty amazing."

She laughed softly. "It was a two-way street. Not every man would have been willing, under those circumstances."

He snorted. "Then you don't know shit about men, honey. I would have stripped naked in the middle of traffic and let the pope watch for the chance to fuck someone like you."

"Someone like me?"

"Yeah. Someone like you." He touched her cheek. "I enjoyed meeting you, Shelby with no last name."

She winced. "We could remedy that."

He shook his head, jingling his keys in his pocket. "No. Let's keep the anonymity. It's probably better that way, and it means I can relegate you to the status of 'most incredible sexual memory.'"

She laughed, flattered in spite of herself. "You're pretty slick. I can't imagine many nights going by without you having a female in your bed."

He rocked back on his heels. "That's where you'd be wrong then. Women almost always want something. I don't have time for that right now. This thing with you was sex for the sake of sex. No strings attached. In guy code, that's pretty close to perfection."

She sighed. "Well, whatever you call it, I still want to say thank you, Jason. I enjoyed myself, and I have a sneaking suspicion that my husband did, too. Though I'm not entirely sure he enjoyed *all* of it," she admitted with wry honesty.

He unlocked his car door. "You'd better not keep him waiting any longer. The guy's been a damned saint, if you ask me."

She looked up at the bedroom window, her smile wistful. "He's an incredible man."

"And a hell of a lucky one." He pulled her close for a long, lazy, thorough kiss.

When they pulled apart, her knees were shaking and Jason looked punchy. He cleared his throat. "Well, be sure to look me up if he ever strays again. I'll be happy to help you even the score."

She nibbled her bottom lip. "I don't think this was about revenge at all. I think I just wanted to try something new."

"And?"

"And now I have," she said simply. "Eric and I are good. He's the man I'm going to spend the rest of my life with."

"Monogamy is a lifetime sentence," he warned, sounding far older and more cynical than his age warranted.

"Spoken like a true bachelor," she teased. "Wait until you fall in love. You'll see."

His face was almost wistful. "I'll take your word for it, pretty Shelby. Good night."

And with no more parting salute than that, he drove out of her life . . . .

Shelby locked up and turned out the lights, pausing to fuss momentarily over a few things in the kitchen. She was apprehensive about returning upstairs. Eric's state of mind was a big fat unknown.

Was he angry? Disgusted? Disappointed in her? While she was in the midst of getting her brains screwed out, it shamed her to know that Eric and his reactions had not even been on her radar.

For the first few minutes . . . sure. But after she and Jason got into it, all she'd been able to do was feel. Was this how men looked at sex? Plain and simple—need meeting need? No hearts and flowers, no messy personal relationships?

In some odd way, this thing with Jason had actually helped her understand Eric's infidelity. He'd been scratching an itch, nothing more.

Of course, some people would argue that he had betrayed his marriage vows. And in truth, when Eric had first confessed, she *had* felt betrayed. Terribly so. But admitting her own culpability had taken some of the sting out of it.

And now that she had experienced sex with a man who wasn't her husband, she could hardly hold Eric's lapse against him anymore.

Tit for tat. Back to normal. Or was it?

She climbed the stairs with her stomach in a knot. The expensive fabric of her negligee slid and swished over her sensitized skin with every step. She felt sexual in a way she hadn't for a long time. Like she could conquer the world, given half a chance.

The lips of her sex tingled and throbbed, making it impossible to think of anything but consummation. She paused in the hallway and then walked quietly into the bedroom.

When she sat down beside Eric, he woke up. He blinked and focused on her face, sleep heavy in his eyes. "Shelby?"

She took his nearest hand in hers. "Why did you decide to join us?"

His eyes darkened. He reared up on his elbows and looked around as though disoriented. "I heard you," he muttered.

She frowned, confused. "Of course you heard us. You were right there beside us sitting in the chair."

He cleared his throat. "Not then. I mean the last time. I slipped out when the two of you fell asleep, but then I heard you. . . ." He stumbled to a halt and sat up, scraping his hair from his forehead.

She winced. "When we did it again."

He leaned back against the headboard, looking anywhere but at her. "Yeah."

She stroked his thigh. "So you wanted me, too. I like that, Eric. It makes me feel wonderful to know you were willing to share the experience. And having both of you at the same time..." Her voice trailed off. She couldn't quite explain what that had been like.

Eric's expression went taut, and somehow she knew it was too soon to talk about the ménage à trois they had shared.

She spoke rapidly, trying to erase the tension between them. "But he's gone now. It's over. No more sex on the side for either of us. From now on, we satisfy each other. No one else. Agreed?"

He frowned. "You didn't enjoy it?"

"Of course I did. You were there. But that's not what I want. I want you. Our marriage. Children."

He stared at her in silence. "I've never seen you like that, Shelby. He made you soar. God knows I want to, but who's to say I can satisfy you like that ever again?" He closed his eyes, his neck bent.

If Eric hadn't looked so miserable, she might have laughed. Instead she stroked his leg. "Don't be a doofus."

His head snapped up and he gaped at her. "What the hell does that mean?"

She smiled gently. "Think about it, Eric.... Nothing you

watched me do tonight with Jason was *Kama Sutra*. It was plain old tab-A-into-slot-B sex. Nothing kinky or fancy."

He frowned. "But I saw you," he insisted doggedly. "When you were with him, you came like firecrackers were exploding inside you. He excited you. Admit it."

She coasted her hand over his balls, his penis. "I was excited, yes. And Jason was a generous lover. But you were responsible for the incredible orgasms."

"Not fucking likely," he said sullenly, his masculine pride in tatters.

She leaned forward and caught his face between her hands. "I don't lie to you, Eric. You know that." She made sure his eyes were locked on hers before she continued. "What made me so excited, so out of control, was knowing that you were watching. Knowing that your cock was hard and weeping and ready to take me over and over again for the rest of the night as soon as I got rid of the second-string guy."

She released him and sat back, studying the play of emotions on his face. Disbelief. Doubt. Hope. And finally . . . gratitude. That last one made her throat close up with hot tears. She had never meant to put him through such torment. It had never once occurred to her that Eric might think her experience of sex with Jason was better or more fulfilling than it was with him. Such a thing was ludicrous.

But then she remembered how her sexual confidence had

wavered in the wake of Eric's confessed infidelity, and suddenly she understood much better.

She smiled softly, her heart full. "You're ignoring the most important part of the evening."

He looked confused.

She sighed, wondering if all men were this obtuse. "When you joined us, sweetheart, the orgasm I had was a thousand times more powerful. Because you were with me. You excite me more than any man ever will or could."

She unfastened the knot in the sash of her robe, letting the sides fall loose. Eric's eyes zeroed in on her partially revealed breasts.

She manufactured a pout. "Are we okay now?"

He looked a bit wary. "Aren't you tired? I don't want to push you."

She shook her head. "Never too tired for you, my love."

Eric remained frozen for all of thirty seconds. Then he shook his head, trying to clear the fog. He still wasn't entirely sure that Shelby wasn't placating him. She had a soft heart. She wouldn't want to hurt his feelings. So she might be covering her real responses, sugarcoating the truth.

But no. Shelby didn't lie. If she said Eric was responsible for the level of her excitement, he should believe her.

He shuddered, feeling his prick thicken and swell. Just having

Shelby's hand on his thigh had been enough to bring him back to attention. He was hard and aching, and so near the edge, it seemed his earlier releases had been only a dream.

He exhaled a soft sigh. In the candlelight, her skin gleamed soft and pure.

His mouth went dry. The temptation to pounce on her almost took over. But he ignored his petulant penis and instead merely touched her hair. He'd always loved Shelby's hair. The pale blond color was natural, and her thick, heavy tresses were as soft as silk.

He tucked a strand behind each ear. Then he pulled her close until every bare inch of her lush, soft body was plastered against every bare inch of his hard, angular body. The contrasts made his head swim.

He explored her like a blind man, relearning the slopes and valleys, lingering over the sensitive spots that made her gasp.

He wanted to show her tenderness, but at the moment he wasn't sure he could maintain a slow, steady loving. A maelstrom of needs rode him hard, not the least of which was the urge to wipe the other man from Shelby's brain. To obliterate any memory she carried of the other man's prick, his scent, his moves.

He kept his expression impassive, but his gut was screaming for him to get on with it. He looked at his wife. And then he deliberately pictured Jason rutting between her legs. The lick of anger gave him the edge he needed.

He narrowed his eyes. "Get on your hands and knees." He

might not be the first man in her bed tonight, but he would be the last.

Her eyelids flickered at his tone, but her cheeks flushed with excitement. She rolled over and put a couple of pillows beneath her tummy, bracing herself on her hands and knees. Deliberately, it seemed, she presented her heart-shaped ass in his direction.

Eric reached for the bedside table and retrieved one of the condoms Jason had left behind, along with some lubricant. The room was still semidark, and it was possible that Shelby didn't see the items he held in his hand.

She knelt motionless, passive, mutely offering her body for his pleasure. He put on the condom and moved behind her, placing a palm on the small of her back. The gentle curve of her hips was poetry.

He reached forward and twined a hank of her hair around his fist. "You enjoyed yourself a bit too much tonight, my horny little wife. I think I might need to punish you."

"You had fun, too," she said, refusing to be dominated just yet.

He spread her knees a fraction more. "Some," he admitted, remembering his last incredible climax. "But I'm not sure the pain was worth it."

"Pain?" she said, her voice uncertain.

"Yeah," he admitted in a ragged voice. "It hurt like hell to see that guy fuck you. And I discovered something about myself."

"Discovered what?"

He dribbled the gel down the crack of her ass. "I discovered

I didn't really like being the other guy in your pussy tonight. I guess I'm more selfish than I thought." He ignored her shocked exclamation and eased the head of his penis into her asshole.

Shelby flinched and protested. "Eric, don't. You know I don't like that."

"Too bad," he said silkily. "Turns out I have a hankering to screw you where nobody else has been. And this would be it."

He pressed a half inch deeper, and Shelby moaned. He wasn't planning to go all the way, but Shelby didn't have to know that.

He squeezed her butt. "You acted the part of a whore tonight, honey. And whores do things that nice little wives don't."

Her shoulders were rigid. "Take it out," she muttered. "Please."

He remained still, but he slid a hand beneath her and found her clit. "If I make you come like this, we'll know, won't we?"

"Know what?" Her voice was a breathless thread.

"That you're a slut who'll take it anywhere."

He kept his hips still and moved his hand. He knew exactly where and how his wife liked to be touched. In seconds she was moaning and pressing against his hand. Her erotic writhing tested his control. "You like being fucked like this," he said. "Admit it."

He pressed deeper and she whimpered. "No, please. I can't come."

"Sure, you can," he said, no sympathy at all in his tone. "Try

harder." He caressed her faster, with just the right pressure. Shelby squirmed and panted, and then without warning her muscles clamped down so hard he was afraid she might crush his prick.

"Eric!" Her shocked cry as she climaxed filled him with satisfaction . . . and massaged his aching cock in amazing ways.

He pulled out and ripped off the condom with shaking hands. With a shout, he entered her again from behind, this time plunging as deep as he was able into her wet pussy.

Shelby jerked and climaxed a second time. He thrust furiously, banging his hips against her ass, filling her so completely, so totally, it seemed that flesh might fuse to flesh.

His arms began to tremble. His fingers dug deep into her ass, and his balls tightened. And finally, he came . . . violently, triumphantly, with such searing force that he saw blackness and tiny yellow stars.

Then he collapsed on top of her and knew no more.

Shelby lay stunned beneath her husband's weight, smiling weakly as she gathered the strength to push him to his side. When she could see his face once again, she touched his cheek tenderly. "Eric?"

He mumbled and opened one eye. "Yeah?"

"I should be angry."

His second eyelid rose. "Oh?"

She leaned over and kissed him full on the mouth. His hands

came up to cup her breasts, and she shivered, looking down at him with a frown. "You totally disregarded my wishes."

He wrinkled his nose. "Sorry about that."

She chuckled. "Really?"

His sheepish grin tipped her off. "No, honey. Not really."

She curled into his side with her head on his chest, listening to the steady thump of his heart. "Well, don't let it happen again."

He pinched her ass. "I'm not making any promises, Shelby, love. Sometime a man's gotta do what a man's gotta do."

She sighed. "You can be a real pain in the ass . . . you know that?"

"Now you're making me hot again," he warned, laughing huskily.

She took him in her hand and squeezed lightly. "That's a naughty thing to say."

He groaned deep in his chest as she worked his burgeoning erection. "Take me or leave me, Shelby."

And moments later . . . with great satisfaction . . . she took him one more time.

TUESDAYS
WITH LORI

Chapter One

Lori Davenport sat in an uncomfortable chair in the lobby of her dentist's office and leafed through a six-month-old issue of *Cosmo*. It was full of ideas for creating special gifts and also making the most of the romantic Christmas season. Maybe if she started now, she might be ready for *next* December.

Or maybe not. She and Kent had more on their plates than they could handle at the moment. Both of them were working long hours to make their dreams come true. It wasn't merely a pie-in-the-sky fantasy. With determination and self-discipline they knew they could make it happen very soon.

Twenty-four months from now they planned to be the proud

owners of a big, rambling farmhouse in the countryside, with a huge yard and maybe even a beagle. Lori would be pregnant with the first of their four children, and their bank account would be healthy enough for her to be a stay-at-home mom.

It was a pretty dream . . . and entirely doable, with a bit of sacrifice. They'd chosen to forgo first-run movies at the theater, expensive dinners out, unnecessary dry cleaning, and a host of other little luxuries that most people took for granted. So far they hadn't missed any of those things too much.

Well, at least, not most of them. One omission really sucked. And Lori wasn't sure if she was willing to give it up for another two years. As much as it pained her to admit it, she and Kent no longer had wild and wonderful sex. Oh, they still had sex. Sure. Two or three times a week.

But it was a fall-into-bed-exhausted kind of thing. Five minutes max, and then lights out. And half the time she was too tired to try for the big O. It was far easier to let Kent do his thing and then cuddle until they both fell asleep.

She glanced at the clock over the front desk and sighed. The only thing worse than having your teeth drilled was having to wait an interminable hour before having your teeth drilled.

She flipped a few more pages, and a bold headline in a fancy font caught her eye. "Is Marriage the Death of Good Sex?"

Oh, my God. Had someone been following her and Kent? Were there hidden cameras in their bedroom? She skimmed the subheadings, looking for some proof that her sex life wasn't the subject of a horrid exposé.

She wasn't sure if she was relieved or depressed to find out that it wasn't. The statistics were impersonal. Apparently no one cared about her and Kent. Apparently many men found the legalities of a marriage certificate about as arousing as oatmeal. Apparently a lackluster sex life was more commonplace than she realized.

She'd heard the jokes, of course. The wife who always had a headache. The husband who bopped a bridesmaid at the wedding reception. But she had never really believed them. In the four years she and Kent had been together, eighteen months of that time married, they had enjoyed sex in every conceivable location, and in a good number of positions as well.

Maybe they weren't Brad and Angelina, but they did okay. Kent knew his way around a woman's body, and she had no complaints.

But if she were brutally honest, the last year and a half had been downhill since the honeymoon. Admitting such blasphemy to herself was so upsetting, she forgot to wince when they called her back and the hygienist started scraping and buffing.

She closed her eyes, not by any means in a position to contemplate romance. But despite the location and the discomfort, her mind went unbidden to thoughts of Kent, her handsome, blond-headed husband. He hated being a couple of inches shy of six feet, but she'd never minded. He still towered over her own five-foot, four-inch stature. And just because he was shorter than some guys, he definitely hadn't been "shorted" in that other most important male category.

The first time she'd seen his penis, she nearly fainted. They hadn't had sex at that point, and she had doubts about whether that thing would fit.

But Kent's wacky sense of humor and down-to-earth sexuality won her over. He had a look in his eyes when he was horny that made a woman melt in all sorts of interesting places.

She'd been fairly inexperienced, and it had been fun to try to keep up with his earthy, sensual lovemaking. Kent didn't know the word *bashful*. And he was up for anything . . . literally.

But sadly, it had been a long, long time since either of them had put sex at the top of the list. They'd made their jobs and their goals a priority.

Eric was a very junior bank manager, but his drive and determination had caused him to move quickly through the ranks with appropriate raises along the way. He had a mind like a calculator, and an easy charm that made him a hit with customers. He didn't bullshit them . . . He gave it to them straight, and they appreciated his blunt advice in money matters.

Lori was content to let Kent handle all the financial details that went with their master plan. She worked freelance as an editor for both college undergrads and grad students. For a fee she would "clean up" papers, and for an even bigger fee, she would take a mess of legal pad pages written in longhand and turn them into a crisp, professional document.

She did some work for faculty as well. She was good, and she was fast, and her reputation had grown in the community. She had more and more work as the months went by.

The downside was that it was hard to pass up a paying job. Near the end of last semester she'd been surviving on four hours of sleep a night in order to take as many projects as possible.

It wasn't unusual for her to work late into the evenings and on weekends. Kent pulled his weight by dealing with the lawn and the bills. They shared shopping, laundry, and meal preparation.

They had their goals in sight at all times, and they agreed on all important issues. On paper, their marriage was steady as a rock.

But they were young and at their physical peak. Was it okay that being sexually adventurous had faded so quickly? Was it really a marriage certificate that had taken the zip out of their intimacy? Or was the fault their own? Had they been so focused on the future that they had shortchanged the present?

An hour later, the torture complete, she wrote a check for her copay and wandered out to the parking lot, lost in thought. The September afternoon was chilly, and a flurry of red and orange leaves danced in a miniwhirlwind in the street.

She drove home in silence, not bothering to turn on the radio. It made her nauseous to ponder the implications of that damned article. Had the damage already been done? Was her marital sex life permanently consigned to the blah column?

The closer she got to home, the madder she got. No way in hell was she giving up on great sex. She and Kent were the perfect couple, and just because they had some pretty conventional dreams didn't mean that their sex lives had to be boring.

Kent was already there when she got home. On Tuesdays he got off at one, because he worked a Saturday shift. More and more banks were going to weekend hours, and as the low man on the totem pole, he was usually the one who had to be there.

He greeted her with a distracted smile, his head bent over the filing cabinet. Kent believed in keeping on top of the paperwork so that when tax time came they would be ready. She'd just as soon toss everything under the bed and hope for the best.

She put away the few groceries she'd stopped for on the way home and checked the phone messages. Then she spent a half hour looking over a new set of assignments. She triaged them, deciding that two of the shorter ones could be knocked out in a morning.

They fixed dinner together, laughing, talking, just like every other day. It was nice. It was comfy. It was freaking unacceptable.

She stewed silently while they cleaned up the dishes. A plan percolated in the back of her mind, but she needed to fine-tune it. Kent went for a run at about seven. Gym memberships weren't in their tight budget, and he liked to stay in shape.

While he was gone, she took a shower and put on her sexiest, slinkiest nightgown. It was pale mauve satin with tiny spaghetti straps. She had washed her hair and blown it dry. Usually she tugged it up in a sloppy ponytail. Tonight she brushed it until it popped and crackled with electricity, and left it to curl loosely on her bare shoulders.

Finally she took one of the ladder-back chairs from the kitchen table, carried it up the stairs to their bedroom, and positioned it right in the middle of the floor. Then she piled the shams and pillows against the headboard, leaned back in a sexy pose, and waited for her unsuspecting husband.

Kent rounded the corner of the last block and sighed with relief as the house came into sight. God, he was tired. A beer and watching the tape of Monday night's football game would do the trick. Maybe he could convince Lori to snuggle on the sofa with him while she read over some papers.

He paused in the kitchen for a drink of water and then sprinted up the stairs, headed for the shower. He stopped dead in the doorway of their bedroom.

"Lori?" His voice ended on an embarrassing squeak. His lovely wife reclined on their bed in a seductive pose, and he was pretty damn sure she had sex on her mind. Suddenly football fell way down the list.

He scratched his chest. "Did I miss something?" Her long, naturally wavy red hair tumbled around her shoulders, and even from this distance he could see her pointy nipples puckering the thin, slick fabric of the nightgown.

She shook her head, her pretty dark green cat eyes sparkling with mischief and challenge. "Go take your shower."

The husky tone in her voice went straight to his dick and made it rise quickly to attention. She noticed, of course.

The sexual chuckle deep in her throat made the hair on the back of his neck stand up.

He dove for the bathroom, stripped off his sweaty running clothes, and ducked under the shower. As he soaped his torso and other areas that he hoped like hell would see some action, his mind stayed focused on the woman in his bed.

Lori was a walking wet dream. He'd been infatuated with her from the first moment they met, and even the fact that she had a half dozen guys panting after her wasn't enough to discourage him. He'd waged an all-out campaign, and when it was over, Lori was his.

She was one of the most innately sexual females he had ever met, but very fastidious when it came to sex and her body. He'd assumed by looking at her that she'd had a few lovers. When he was privileged to be invited into her bed, he discovered that beneath the sensual exterior was a very private, surprisingly innocent woman.

If he hadn't already been head over heels in love with her, he would have fallen hard the first night they made love. Lori had reveled in everything about their mating; her enthusiasm and willingness to learn were powerful aphrodisiacs. Her curvy body and pale skin were the perfect foils for her vibrant red hair. She resembled one of those lush courtesans in old paintings.

He'd been drunk on sex that night . . . the smell of it, the taste of it, the incredible feel of her skin beneath his hands. She had a Kathleen Turner kind of voice, making every husky laugh, every double entendre a sexual challenge.

There were many days when he stopped and thanked God that some other guy hadn't found her first.

He shut off the water and toweled dry, scraping his hands through his short hair in lieu of a comb. He shrugged into his navy terry robe and opened the bathroom door.

He almost swallowed his tongue. Lori was touching herself. One hand played with her breasts. The other rubbed lightly between her legs. The gown was still in place. Where she fondled her pussy, a damp spot darkened the material, revealing her excitement.

He strode toward the bed, but she stopped him with one up-raised, imperious hand. "No. Sit in the chair. And lose the robe."

For the first time he noticed the one piece of furniture so oddly out of place. He lifted an eyebrow. "Why?"

Apparently he wasn't supposed to ask questions. Her brows narrowed. "Because I said so."

He grinned. "Yes, ma'am." He dropped the robe and sat, as she had commanded.

Lori stood up, drawing his attention to the sleek, voluptuous lines of her body. Not much was hidden in the skimpy gown she wore.

When she got close enough, he could smell the fragrance of her shower gel, as well as the perfume she had applied afterward. His nose—and his cock—twitched in appreciation.

He grabbed for her hand. "Wanna sit in my lap, little girl?"

She batted his arm away. "Sit still." She moved behind him, and he heard a drawer open.

Without any protest from him she drew his hands behind his back, and suddenly he felt the cold bite of metal against his wrists. "Hey," he said, jerking away just a half second too late. That split-second delay meant he was now firmly secured to the chair with what he knew to be regulation handcuffs. A buddy of his from college, now a cop, had given him a pair at his bachelor party, and at one time Kent and Lori had fooled around with them quite a bit.

But that had been ages ago.

He twisted his hands experimentally. Yup. Trussed like a wino waiting to be thrown into the tank.

He felt Lori's hands settle on his shoulders. She massaged the muscles in his neck lightly. Then she leaned close to his head and spoke quietly. "Kent . . . I'm not happy with our sex life."

Wow. A knife to the gut would have left less of a mark. He cleared his throat. "I see." And then he frowned. "We had sex three times last week."

More of the gentle massage. "I'm not talking about quantity," she whispered, her breath tickling his ear. "You're the man who taught me that sex is one of life's greatest pleasures. But we've gotten lazy. 'Slam, bam, thank you, ma'am' is not exactly romantic."

He relaxed. Ah, so this was about romance. He *had* been a little lax in that department lately. Tomorrow he'd stop somewhere and get flowers to bring home. Lori sure as hell deserved them.

She ran her hands through his hair and massaged his scalp, making his neck tingle. "I've been making some plans, Kent. Things are going to be different around here from now on. And I hope you'll be on board with all I have in mind."

Still, her fingers worked their magic. "Sure, honey. Why wouldn't I be?"

She left him and went to sit on the end of the bed, her hands in her lap. Her feet were flat on the floor, and her eyes were dark emerald and deadly serious. "We are far too young to settle for ho-hum sex. We've only been husband and wife for eighteen months, and already we're in a rut. Does being married make me less sexy to you?"

He gawked at her. "You're kidding, right? You're the sexiest woman I've ever met. Why do you think I married you?"

She shrugged her narrow shoulders once, her expression pensive. "I don't know. But some men find that being legally tied down takes some of the fun out of the bedroom."

He swore under his breath, realizing suddenly that this was more than just feminine pique. Lori was genuinely worried. "Well, I'm not one of them," he said forcefully, wishing he were free to go to her and hug her. "I *want* to be tied to you. Permanently. And I won't ever stop wanting your luscious body."

"Even when I'm using a walker?" she teased, her face lighter now.

"Will you bend over when you hang on to it?" he deadpanned.

Her mouth fell open, and then she laughed, her cheeks turning pink. "That's disrespectful, Mr. Davenport. Shame on you."

He wagged his dick at her. "I am what I am, little girl."

Her eyes glazed over for a second, fixed on his eager erection. Then she licked her lips and refocused her attention on his face. "Well, uh . . ."

"Undo these cuffs, Lori," he said urgently. "I want to screw you."

She shook her head regretfully. "No. Sorry. That's not part of the plan."

It was his turn to frown. "So far your plan sucks. I love the bondage thing as much as the next guy, Lori, believe me, but this conversation has made me horny. I want to touch you."

She pursed her lips. "Once upon a time everything made you horny. What happened?"

He moved uneasily. "I still get horny. But I can't exactly walk around with a boner at work."

She cocked her head. "I wonder . . ."

He could barely hear the speculative words. She seemed to be speaking to herself. He spoke loudly, demanding her attention. "You wonder what?"

She shook her head as though clearing it of excess thoughts. "Nothing. Never mind."

Then she astounded him by standing up and stripping off her gown. *Hot damn.* Now she was going to straddle his lap. . . .

But apparently not. She leaned over the bed, giving him a great view from behind of her pink pussy lips. She grabbed a couple of pillows and positioned them near the end of the bed. Then she sat back down, scooted back on the spread, and got comfortable with her shoulders raised and supported and one knee bent.

Sweet holy hell. Now all he needed was a *Penthouse* photographer to record the moment. She looked fuckin' awesome. He cleared his throat. "You look amazing, Lori. Uncuff me and I'll take your picture."

She appeared to be ignoring him. Her head lolled back on the pillows, her eyelids fluttered shut, and her right hand glided down over her belly and settled between her legs. He was starting to get a bad feeling about this. "Lori?"

No response. His wife's nimble fingers parted her own slick folds and began a slow, erotic movement back and forth over her clitoris.

He sucked in a breath. "Damn, honey. I'd be honored to help you with that. Lori . . . sweetheart."

She was miles away, her lips softly parted, little murmurs escaping her mouth as she pressed and stroked. Her face was flushed and her tongue traced her upper teeth as she began to twist and squirm.

Shit. His dick was a fiery iron poker, straining toward the bed like a hound dog after a bitch in heat. His eyelids were wide-open, all the spare skin on his body stretched tight over his cock.

He growled deep in his chest. "Lori. God, honey. Have mercy."

He was wasting his breath. Her hips lifted. Her hand moved faster and faster. Her slender thighs fell apart, and he could see the moisture gathering beneath her agile fingers.

He wanted to howl in frustration. He wanted to break the damned chair in a million pieces. But most of all, he wanted to bury himself in his wife's hot, tight pussy. He was practically hyperventilating.

He gave up trying to get her attention, and instead slumped back to enjoy the show. There was something to be said for voyeurism. When he was in the midst of making love to his lovely wife, he was too involved to fully appreciate her sensuality from a strictly aesthetic standpoint.

Watching her now, seeing the color in her skin, the eroticism in her movements . . . hearing the sexy little sounds she uttered made him appreciate the whole picture. Every male hormone in his body responded on a visceral level.

His mind might be enjoying the artistic beauty of the scene, but his cock just wanted relief. She was panting now. Nearing the end.

His breath came harder. His heart beat faster. Sweat broke out on his forehead. His arms quivered, and blood pulsed in his prick. It was as though he were inside Lori's skin experiencing the imminent explosion.

He winced, aching from head to toe. His erection was hard as a rock, painfully engorged. He jerked in vain against the stupid cuffs, bruising his wrists.

He'd give anything he owned to be right there beside her, ready to shove deep inside her cunt the moment she climaxed. He loved timing his first forceful thrust at just the right moment to make her come a second time, usually with even more fireworks than the first.

"Lori," he ground out, knowing it was useless, but lost to logic or reason. "Come on, baby, let me in the game," he pleaded hoarsely.

He could see every inch of her glistening pink flesh. Her sweet, womanly smell filled the air. He started to curse, a long, inventive string of random words that didn't even come close to expressing the depths of his frustration and lust.

Her back arched. Her upper teeth bit down on her bottom lip. Her fingers slowed . . . pressed once . . . twice . . . and then Lori cried out and trembled in the grip of what was clearly a bone-deep, intense, and very satisfying orgasm.

Chapter Two

He watched her moan quietly as the last ripples of pleasure slid through her body. Her face was soft, replete with satisfaction. A tiny smile tilted the corners of her mouth.

He gave her maybe sixty more seconds, and then his patience wore thin. "Nice show, Lori. Now let me go. I mean it."

Her eyelashes fluttered open, and her emerald eyes were hazy and unfocused. She licked her lips and sat up, entirely unselfconscious, as far as he could tell, about either her nudity or her performance.

She yawned with a ladylike hand over her mouth, and then

stretched, making her tits rise and fall with mesmerizing effect. "I'll be right back."

"Damn it to hell." But his protest fell on deaf ears. He heard water running in the bathroom, listened to the toilet flush, and plotted all the ways he was going to exact his revenge.

When she reappeared she was wearing a simple white cotton robe.

She stood in the bathroom doorway and studied his predicament. "Quit pulling on your arms," she said quietly. "You know you can't get loose."

"So help me, God," he said between clenched teeth. "You're going to get spanked for this."

Her lips quirked. "It's possible."

She crossed the room and stood in front of him for about two seconds, her gaze drifting from his shoulders to his straining dick and back to his face. Then she sat gracefully at his feet, criss-crossed her legs, propped her elbows on her knees, and rested her chin in her hands. She was so close he could feel her breath on his knees. His cock quivered and his balls tightened.

He touched her knee with his foot. "Now will you let me go?" He made his voice as meek and reasonable as possible.

She tilted her head, her gaze assessing his state of mind. "You said you were on board for anything," she reminded him gently. "Did you forget so soon?"

She took his foot in her hand and began to massage his

instep. Prickles of fire streaked from his arch up his calf to his balls. He squirmed uncomfortably. "I didn't forget," he panted. "I thought you meant fun sex. I'm here to tell you, hon, this ain't fun."

She switched her attentions to his other foot. The muscles in his leg quivered with the effort of blocking the searing currents of sensation.

She finally abandoned the foot torture and placed her hands on the insides of his knees. He hissed and cursed as she accidentally brushed his cock. Or at least, he thought it was an accident. The little smile on her face said otherwise.

Her thumbs rubbed the inner rims of his kneecaps. "Here's the plan, Kent. From now on, every Tuesday afternoon in this house will be about sex. No responsibilities, no chores, no phone calls. Just hot, sweaty, all-out bedroom Olympics."

He swallowed hard. *Hot damn.* Today was Tuesday. "Okay, Lori. Whatever you say."

Her thumbs moved an inch up his thighs, and he forgot to breathe. "You've been the person handling all the details about our future plans. I've decided that it's only fair for me to be in charge of the present plans. Do you have a problem with that?"

He shook his head fervently. "Hell, no."

She nodded and removed her hands. He almost cried.

She took a deep breath. "Well, then. Here are the rules. Every Tuesday you're to come straight home from work, stopping only to grab something for lunch at a drive-through. When you walk in the front door, go straight to the shower, clean up, and wait for me on the bed."

His eyes were glued to her face. The movement of her lips as she spoke was almost hypnotic. "I can do that," he whispered, his throat dry.

She trapped his hungry gaze with her implacable one. "From then on, everything that happens will be up to me. You'll participate, of course, but I'll take the lead. Are we clear?"

He nodded jerkily. "Are we talking S and M?"

She frowned. "Not necessarily. Each week will take a different course. If I do my job well, you won't be able to anticipate my intentions. Surprise will be the key, and the delicious element of anticipation."

She paused, and for a moment he saw once more the faint unease on her face. She sighed. "I will never again settle for ho-hum, scratch-an-itch sex. I want you, Kent, to wake up craving sex . . . and later fall asleep craving sex. I want you to feel your undershorts rubbing against your balls and think of sex. I want you to smell cinnamon or vanilla or lemon or the scent of my arousal and think about sex."

He tried to speak, but his lips were numb.

She smiled gently, seeing his distress. "I want every note of music, every taste of food, every beautiful movie you watch or fascinating book you read to make you think of sex." Her hands went back to his knees. She stroked lazily with her thumbs. Her eyes met his, filled with hot emerald sparks. "I want you addicted, Kent. To me. To fucking. To climaxing. I want you absolutely, forever and ever a slave to that incredible moment when our two bodies join and your prick explodes so hard that you forget your name."

She rocked back on her heels and settled on her butt, lying down gracefully and spreading her thighs wide. She reached for her pussy. He flinched when she propped her feet on his knees. She moved aside the folds of her robe and he could see that she was wet and ready, totally aroused by their conversation. This time there was no desultory buildup. Her hand moved rapidly, her neck went taut, her back arched, and in no time at all a choked scream escaped her lips and she shattered in the throes of a climax that was as beautiful as it was torturous, at least to him.

It took her several minutes to recover. She curled on her side, panting.

"Now, Lori," he said urgently. "Now. I get the picture. And you're right. Let me show you how hungry I am."

She rolled to her knees and fastened the sash of her robe. "No," she said simply.

He jerked as if she had slapped him. "What the hell do you mean, no? This isn't funny." His voice rose an octave, and he didn't care. Lust and fury choked him, and a red haze obscured his vision.

She stood up, her gaze almost sympathetic. "We start next Tuesday. That gives us a week to truly appreciate what it is that we love about sex."

"You can't be serious."

She nodded slowly. "For the next seven nights I'll be sleeping in the guest room with the door locked. It would be too easy to start something while we're half-asleep, so it's better this way."

"Lori . . ." Temper choked him, destroying his reason. "This has gone far enough. No way. I didn't sign on for a case of blue balls."

"You promised," she said simply. "During the week we can kiss if you want to, but don't think you'll seduce me into changing my mind. I won't. Whether or not you jerk off is up to you. If you can't stand the temptation, go ahead. In fact, you might perform better next Tuesday if you've taken the edge off."

The phrase he said was one he'd never used in her presence.

She winced. "I'm sorry if I've made you angry, but this is too important to take lightly. I'm willing to make sacrifices for our future, but giving up sex isn't one of them."

"We have sex, goddammit!" he yelled, goaded beyond endurance.

Her eyes teared up, and it felt as if she had stabbed a knife straight into his heart. "We've been going through the motions," she muttered. "And it just isn't enough, not anymore."

In silence she stepped behind him, and he felt her press the keys to the cuffs into his palm. She must have known that it would take him a few minutes to maneuver at this tricky angle.

She walked to the door. "Good night, Kent. I'll see you in the morning."

He sat perfectly still for over a minute, numb from head to toe except for the throbbing pain in his cock. He was literally speechless. Stunned. Furious. But impotent in his anger. If he continued to protest, she would think he was a selfish bastard.

Suddenly seven days seemed like an eternity. He'd never survive. He'd be stark, raving, slobbering-in-the-street bonkers.

Part of him wanted to yell at her and rant and bitch until she relented in tears. Part of him admired her *cojones*. His little wife had guts—that was for sure. When he allowed himself to think about the following Tuesday, his pulse went haywire.

Clumsily he twisted and jiggled the keys, gnawing on his lip. He held his breath until he felt and heard the little click that signaled his release.

He brought his aching arms in front of him and shook them until the blood surged back into every burning fingertip. He tossed the cuffs and keys aside and started to stand up, but his knees buckled. Maybe he should sit a minute.

He felt like he had the flu. His skin was ice-cold, but he was burning up inside. His head ached, but not nearly as much as his cock. He groaned and dropped his head to his chest. He took his prick in his hands and squeezed gently. A drop of precome glistened on the head. It hurt to touch himself.

He felt like one of those ads for male enhancement pills. . . . *Warning: Any erection lasting over four hours may need medical attention.* His short, sharp laugh held no amusement. It hadn't been four hours yet, but given the week to come, he just might end up in the emergency room. He had a feeling that all the hand jobs in the world weren't going to appease this burning ache.

Gritting his teeth against the painfully sensitive experience of caressing his own flesh, he started a rhythmic pull and tug. He'd been locked in sexual frustration for so long, he wanted to make this last, needed to experience a long, satisfying climb to the top. But that wasn't going to happen.

In seconds his hips were straining forward, his chest was heaving, and then in an almost blackout moment of release, he came in three hard, draining spurts. Even as sticky white semen trickled over his thighs, his prick remained semihard.

He thought about Lori's vow, her dogged determination to make them both wait, and he wanted to crawl on his hands and knees to her bed across the hall and beg for one last fuck to hold him over.

But he didn't waste his time. His wife was bullheaded and focused and not about to give up on something she felt was important. Which left him up shit creek without a paddle, as his daddy used to say. He staggered to the bathroom and washed up.

He walked across the hall, still nude, and knocked softly on the guest room door. No light leaked from beneath the door. No soft, welcoming voice bade him enter.

He jiggled the doorknob. "Lori? Are you awake?"

Silence. He leaned against the smooth wood and bumped his

head lightly on the raised panel. "Are you sure about this?" He thought he could smell her perfume. Was she ignoring him or was she asleep?

She'd had two spectacular orgasms in the last hour, so maybe she'd drifted off without a care in the world. Thinking about his wife in the throes of climax was a mistake. His semierect penis, always hopeful, sprang to attention once again.

He cursed. "Lori?" *Shit.* A man's pride could take only so much abuse. He waited for one last hopeful minute, but the deafening quiet defeated him. He returned to the lonely master bedroom, climbed between the covers, and tried to sleep.

When Lori went down to the kitchen the next morning, Kent was already there. She had dressed purposely in the least sexy things she owned—a ratty college sweatshirt, baggy jeans, and thick socks. It was pretty much the outfit she'd worn every time she'd pulled an all-nighter before an exam.

Kent was at the stove, frying bacon. He looked up with no expression whatsoever on his face, but his eyes were watchful. "Two eggs?"

She nodded. She found the loaf of bread and put two pieces at a time in the toaster. It was a familiar morning routine. By the time she had poured each of them a glass of juice and a cup of coffee, the scrambled eggs were ready. They sat down at the table together and began to eat.

She couldn't think of a single thing to say. Kent wolfed down his food and then stared at her while she picked at hers.

He cocked his head. "Not hungry?"

She squirmed in her seat. There was an edge to his voice that suggested his anger still simmered on a slow burn. She had never intended to make him mad. She'd been going for rabidly horny. But she should have remembered that in the male of the species, deferred lust had a nasty bite. She forced herself to swallow another bite of eggs and then put down her fork with a sigh. "Not really," she admitted.

Kent filched her last piece of bacon. "How did you sleep last night?" he asked, watching her face as he chewed.

She felt her cheeks flame red. The silky sarcasm in his pointed question dredged up a ton of guilt. Thanks to her two self-induced orgasms, she'd slept like a baby. From Kent's tone of voice and the dark circles under his eyes, she guessed he hadn't fared as well.

Sometime around midnight she had slipped across the hall to make sure he'd been able to get the cuffs undone. It had occurred to her during one panicked moment of self-doubt that he might have dropped the keys and been in there still chained to the chair.

But their bedroom was dark and the chair had disappeared. She stood in the doorway for several long minutes, listening to the quiet sounds of his breathing. Already her bed in the guest room seemed cold and lonely. Six more nights of her self-imposed exile would seem infinitely long.

She stood up and carried her dishes to the sink. "I slept great," she said, keeping all inflection from her voice.

"I'll bet you did," he muttered, joining her at the counter and using the sprayer to rinse his plate.

When they were finished putting everything away, Kent leaned against the fridge and gave her that intent, heated stare that was beginning to make her nervous. "I probably won't come home after work," he said. "I may go play poker with the guys."

She nodded slowly. "Okay. That's fine. What about dinner?"

His lips twisted. "I'll grab something out. Don't wait up for me."

She took a half step forward, suddenly upset. Was this how Kent was planning to deal with her no-sex ultimatum? Was he simply going to make himself scarce until next Tuesday?

She put her hands on her hips. "If that's what you want," she said quietly, a little disappointed. She worked alone at home all day. She wasn't looking forward to spending the evenings by herself as well.

A look of pure male frustration flashed across his face, and he crossed the room in two long strides. He took her shoulders in his hands and shook her, not hard enough to hurt, but with enough restrained energy to let her see his annoyance. "This is what I want," he hissed.

His mouth covered hers and his tongue thrust deep between

her lips. Her sex clenched as a fresh wave of arousal stabbed deep in her belly. He ground his hips into hers, pressing his erection against her mound.

One of his big hands went beneath her sweatshirt and found her bare breast. He pinched her nipple, making her knees buckle as she gasped and whimpered. His free hand slid down the front of her loose jeans and cupped her between her legs. His thumb found her clitoris and pressed lightly.

She tried to push him away. "No. We have to wait," she pleaded.

He nibbled her ear. "I may not be fucking you for six more days," he muttered against her neck, "but I sure as hell will play with my wife's pussy any damn time I please." And then, with a masterful stroke that left her gasping, he replaced his thumb with two talented fingers and sent her tumbling into bliss.

She was still shivering with aftershocks when he left the room. *Damn.* If she had expected her husband to stand by passively for the next six days, she'd been sorely mistaken. He'd copped an attitude about her whole plan, and she wasn't sure whether she liked it or not.

On the one hand, his state of mind said that he was definitely thinking about sex. But on the other hand, his almost belligerent demeanor made her wonder if next Tuesday's program would be easy to carry out. She had visions of him tumbling her on the kitchen table before she even got a chance to do all the naughty things she was planning.

It was a measure of how much she wanted to feel his thick length between her legs that she actually considered abandoning her plan. But no. She was right to want to spice things up. Even her little confrontation the night before had already notched up the sexual tension in the house by about ten degrees. How much hotter would they both be after a week of self-denial?

Kent left without his usual good-bye kiss. She found the front door ajar and heard the squeal of tires as he rounded the sharp curve at the end of the street. She prayed fervently that his sexual frustration wouldn't impair his driving ability too much.

She spent four hours doggedly working through a pile of projects. Then she ate a quick sandwich for lunch and went into the den to sit down at the computer. Her pocketbook was on the desk beside her. She pulled out her credit card and flipped it over and over in her hand for several long minutes.

She and Kent, as part of their master plan, had agreed that neither of them would make any unnecessary purchases over fifty dollars without discussing it with each other first. They had adhered to that agreement religiously.

What would happen if Lori deliberately ignored their pact and spent a reckless amount of money to fund her sexual fantasies? Would Kent appreciate her dedication to the sensual arts, or would he be pissed?

With a Scarlett O'Hara toss of the head, she placed the credit card beside the mouse pad and Googled *sex toys* and another phrase even more explicit. The sites that popped up were both educational and titillating. She reached for a pad of paper and began making notes.

Kent wondered how badly he could perform and still keep his job. So far he had made three fairly serious mistakes, and it was only noon. He'd tried every concentration technique he knew, but none of them worked. All he could think about was having sex with Lori next Tuesday.

His computer screen saver might as well have been a photo of his nude wife crying out in climax. That was all he could see when he looked at the computer monitor anyway—her fiery hair, her pale skin, her teasing green eyes filled with mischief and resolve. God, he was in bad shape. He went from anger to lust to amused tenderness to shivering anticipation in endless dizzy circles.

His little "hand in the pants" routine that morning had been a slip. He was determined to prove that he could hold out a week if Lori could. But hell, he was in bad shape, and it had been less than a day. What kind of condition would he be in by next Monday night?

When he got his mind off the thought of actually fucking Lori, he found himself snared in the contemplation of what his naughty wife might choose to spice up their sex life. Truthfully, he was still a bit hurt. For a marriage of a mere eighteen months already to be blah in the bedroom was sobering. And he should and would take most or all of the blame.

He'd been pushing Lori hard and working hard himself. He had a streak of type A workaholic a mile wide, and he'd patted himself on the back metaphorically as he watched their bank balance grow. Their goals were shared, true. But he'd dragged Lori along in his dogged determination to get there fast, and he had never really given her a chance to protest.

In his mind there had always been plenty of time in the future for other things, but obviously Lori wasn't prepared to wait. His wife was pretty damned insightful. He hadn't realized until last night how complacent he had become about sex.

He and Lori had lived together for two years before they got married. But sharing an apartment had a whole different dynamic from standing in front of God and everybody on both sides of their families and pledging the "till death do us part" stuff.

Before they got married, he had been on his best behavior. He'd still been a little incredulous that this gorgeous, fabulous woman was willing for him to screw her at will. He'd delighted in showing her any number of naughty and inventive—even shocking to Lori—lovemaking positions and techniques.

But by the time they got married two years later, maybe he had begun taking their sex life for granted. She deserved better. Hell, *he* deserved better. And it had taken only this little wake-up call to make him realize what he had been doing.

Knowing he could go home every night to his nice warm house and get fucked by his nice hot wife was pretty much a dream come true. And as with many wonderful things that came too easily, perhaps he'd become blasé.

Just the mere suggestion of not having sex for seven days had sent him into a tailspin. When he knew he could have sex any night he wanted it, he'd been content with a late-night tumble to get his rocks off. He wasn't selfish. He always made sure Lori was satisfied. But for a long time now, he truly hadn't given a thought to being creative beneath the sheets.

Most nights he'd been bone-weary exhausted. Not that it was an excuse, but he'd been dedicated to their goals and dreams. They both wanted kids, and they both wanted Lori to have the chance to be a full-time mom. She'd be an incredible mother.

Imagining her pregnant with a rounded belly and lush, full tits gave him the weirdest combination of feelings. He felt guilty for being turned on by that mental image, but he'd thought about it a lot lately.

At five sharp he shut down his computer and cleared his desk. There was no poker game. He planned to linger over dinner somewhere and then drive around for a while. He had tennis shoes and grunge clothes in a duffel bag in his trunk, so he could always go to the track at the high school and run laps. Anything to postpone the moment when he had to go home and pretend he wasn't so horny he could die.

God knew what he would do this weekend without work to keep him occupied. His Saturday shift at the bank lasted only from eight until noon. Mowing the grass would chew up another couple of hours, but it was supposed to rain. *Oh, Lord.* Thinking about a lazy rainy afternoon cooped up in the house with Lori made his hands shake.

He'd have to think of something. He was determined to be strong. Hell, all kinds of men existed without sex. Priests. Prisoners. Military men. Of course, the priests had been known to find satisfaction in perverse ways, as had the prisoners. And the military guys, at least the ones without a backbone, probably had a hooker or two on the side. It was the honorable ones who suffered. And if some poor schmuck in a hellhole on the far side of the globe could be celibate and wait for his wife, then Kent could, too.

But at least the military men had hard, sweaty work to keep them busy, and their wives and girlfriends were half a world away.

Kent's temptation was close and available and warm and sexy. . . . *Oh, shit.* He tossed his briefcase in the backseat of his car and ripped off his tie.

Once out on the open road, he eased his foot down on the gas pedal and gripped the steering wheel. *No sex. No sex. No sex.*

Maybe if he said it enough, his prick would finally understand those two simple words.

But as he glanced down at the erection tenting his dress slacks, he doubted it.

Chapter Three

———❦———

Lori stared at the total in her electronic shopping cart and winced—$323.79. Who knew sexual experimentation was so darned expensive? She debated which of the various items she could delete. The nipple clamps? No . . . Kent had mentioned those on several occasions.

What about the swimsuit-style body wear made of black feathers? It was pretty expensive. And it might make her look like a black Donald Duck. But no . . . she had a hankering to see Kent's face when she stroked him with her feathers.

She sighed. There really wasn't a single thing on the list that she was willing to part with. She moved the cursor over the PLACE ORDER button, closed her eyes, and clicked.

Friday she hovered near the front door repeatedly, watching for the deliveryman. She had paid for two-day shipping, and she wanted to bring the package in and hide it before Kent got home from work.

At five after five a brown van pulled into the driveway. She knew she was blushing when she signed the little window on the order-tracking device. The driver was completely uninterested in the contents of her boxes—both of them. He sat them in the foyer, gave her a brief wave, and headed back to his truck.

She balanced one on top of the other and carried them upstairs to the guest room. The closet in that room was used for out-of-season clothes, so she tucked her new, as-yet-unexamined toys beneath and behind some long winter coats and closed the door.

She returned to the kitchen and put the finishing touches on the dinner she had painstakingly prepared. She hoped she and Kent could manage to carry on a civil conversation. Wednesday night she had been in bed by the time he got home from his poker game. Thursday night he settled himself in front of the TV after dinner and barely moved until midnight.

Tonight she was determined to make him acknowledge her presence. What good was sexual tension if the stubborn man wouldn't even look at her?

He walked in the front door at six on the dot. He seemed tired, but his face lit up when he smelled what was cooking. "Chocolate cake?" The look on his face was endearingly hopeful.

Men were like little boys where their stomachs were concerned.

She went to him and kissed his cheek. "Yep. And all your other favorites as well. I decided we might as well appease *one* of your appetites."

She'd decided it was okay to joke about their self-imposed celibacy. Apparently not.

Kent froze. His eyes flared with heat. His briefcase fell to the floor with a thud. Before she could register what was happening, he dragged her hard against his chest and found her mouth.

Sweet heaven. Her knees went weak and she leaned into him. He tasted so damned good. They hadn't kissed in three days, and she was starved for this closeness. She could feel his heart hammering in his chest. His tongue dueled with hers, staking a claim, registering his intent. She opened her mouth wider, feeling the press of his erection between them.

Suddenly she wanted him inside her so badly, the yearning stole her breath. The Tuesday idea was silly anyway. Who cared what day it was?

She felt for his belt buckle. "I can't stand it, Kent. I need you."

He grabbed her hand and held it away from his body. He released her and stepped back, wiping his mouth and breathing in jerky gasps. "No."

She was so aroused, she didn't understand at first. Kent had never turned her down. "No?" she asked blankly, feeling sluggish and stupid.

He glared at her. "It was your idea, Lori. Remember? Seven days of cold turkey? And we haven't even made it halfway through the week."

She stripped off her top and bra, right down to bare skin, feeling desperate. "I don't know what I was thinking," she muttered. "We'll never make it. I need you. Now."

She tried to nuzzle against his chest again, but he dodged her, his wary gaze glued to her naked breasts. "No," he said hoarsely. "You said you wanted me to be starved for sex, aching and desperate. Remember?" The determination in his voice was wavering.

She pouted, fingering her nipples. "Well, aren't you? Starving, I mean."

For one long, heated moment it was a face-off. She watched the struggle on her husband's face, and the hunger she saw there mirrored her own. But he shook his head hard, closing his eyes and clenching his fists at his sides. "Yes," he ground out. "I'm starving. But I agreed to your original plan, and we're sticking to it. No sex, Lori. Not until Tuesday."

Dinner had to be reheated twice. Kent left the house and went running without even poking his head in the kitchen. When he returned an hour later, he headed upstairs for a shower, possibly a cold one.

Lori sublimated her need for sex by scrubbing down all the kitchen cabinets and countertops. When the job was done, she was as horny as ever, but at least she was exhausted.

Kent appeared in the kitchen just before eight o'clock. He gave her a sheepish smile and sat down at the table. They ate in silence, but it was a comfortable, albeit loaded silence.

He complimented her on the roast beef and mashed potatoes. He ate the broccoli without complaint, and when they were both finished, she served the cake.

Some people considered chocolate a decent substitute for sex. Lori had never put it to the test, but after consuming a thick wedge of the decadent dessert, she still wanted to jump her husband's bones. She wasn't sure all the Godivas in the world would be enough to appease her at this very moment.

She stood up to retrieve the bottle of wine from where they had left it on the counter. As she brushed past Kent's shoulder, she couldn't resist touching his hair. He had the thickest, most beautiful hair she had ever seen on a man, and she loved to run her fingers through it. He flinched when she touched him, but his hand came up to cover hers.

She stood there at his side for a full minute, her heart contracting. He leaned his head against her arm, and she bent to kiss his crown. "I love you," she whispered. "You're the best thing in my life."

He captured her wrist and brought it to his lips, brushing the sensitive skin where her pulse beat with a warm kiss. "You *are* my life," he said simply.

After they finished in the kitchen, she joined him in their cozy den and curled up beside him on the soft leather sofa. Normally he would have put an arm around her. Tonight he barely even noticed she was beside him, or so it seemed.

After thirty minutes he got to his feet, his hands stuffed in his pockets. A blotch of red stained each of his cheekbones, and his expression was strained. "I can't do this," he said with a grimace. "I didn't know it was possible to want you as much as I do right now."

She opened her mouth to speak, but he stopped her with an upraised hand. "No. Don't say anything. I'll survive. But I can't sit here with you. I'm sorry." And he disappeared upstairs.

She turned off all the lights and checked the locks before following him. In the hallway outside their bedroom, she stopped to listen. The door was ajar, as was the bathroom door on the far wall. She could hear water running, but another faint sound piqued her curiosity. She eased inside the bedroom, leaving the door exactly the same as she found it. She didn't want to be caught spying on her husband.

She paused outside the bathroom and stood quietly. Over the sound of the rushing water, she heard something else. Kent was jerking off. He made little moans and grunts. Knowing that he was playing with himself because he wanted to be with her gave Lori a funny feeling in the pit of her stomach.

For a moment she contemplated stripping and joining him. If she timed it exactly right, he wouldn't be able to resist. He would back her against the wall of the shower, lift her legs around his waist, and . . .

She closed her eyes, feeling the sharp ache of desire. She imagined her husband's slick, wet, muscular body. He would be hard all over, ready to lift her and take her over and over....

She took one step forward, and suddenly the water turned off. In her heated fantasizing, she had missed the moment of his release. *Damn.*

She stepped lightly but quickly across the carpet and escaped to her new room, her heart beating quickly. That had been close.

She closed her door quietly and leaned against it, looking around her self-imposed prison with a frown. She didn't want to sleep alone tonight. But if her noble husband was going to prove his self-control, it appeared she had no choice.

Kent didn't even mind going in to work on Saturday morning. Anything to stay out of temptation's way. Until now, he'd considered himself a pretty rational, self-controlled guy. But he was rapidly realizing that where his beautiful titian-haired wife was concerned, he was no better than a hungry junkyard dog, waiting for a few scraps to be thrown his way.

He made it through that day and the next by taking the coward's way out—avoidance. It was the only foolproof way to ensure that he wouldn't jump his wife in a weak moment. Lori had begun giving him those big-eyed hurt looks whenever they happened to be in the same room at the same time for a brief moment.

Well, that was just too damned bad. He couldn't play the affectionate husband, given the way he was feeling at the moment.

Her plan had worked even better than she could have imagined. He was not only thinking about sex every minute of the day, but realizing that he had a deep, disturbing capacity for dark-edged lust.

The need to screw Lori was so intense, it almost frightened him. Even though he had agreed to their little game, and even though he had insisted they continue to wait when Lori herself had wavered, anger rolled and twisted like a nasty serpent in his stomach.

He was accustomed to making love to his wife and experiencing warm, fuzzy, affectionate emotions. Nothing about the stabbing torment in his gut was soft or sweet. He wanted to conquer, to dominate, to imprint himself on her delicate flesh. He wanted to bury his aching cock so deeply inside her that she would never again feel whole without him in her pussy.

And the very depth and intensity of those sharp, violent emotions scared him to death.

So he kept his distance and waited with stoic determination for Tuesday to finally come.

Lori never knew how they made it through the weekend. The atmosphere in the house was as oppressive as the heavy, dank air before a storm. By Sunday evening they were snapping and sniping at each other like competitive siblings with something to prove.

On Monday Kent came home from work, changed clothes,

and appeared downstairs with an overnight bag in his hand. He gave her a level stare. "I'll see you tomorrow. I'm staying at a motel tonight."

"With another woman?" Even as the flippant words left her lips, she knew she had made a serious mistake. The incredulous anger on his face sent a rough shiver down her spine.

He dropped his bag on a chair and approached her. "Take it back," he snarled.

She crossed her arms at her waist, biting her lower lip to keep it from trembling. "What else am I supposed to think? You have a perfectly good bed upstairs."

He backed her against the wall, his hips pressing into hers. His breath was hot on her face. Sparks of fire flashed in his azure eyes. "Take . . . it . . . back," he hissed.

Her own frustrated lust boiled to the surface. "It's a legitimate question," she said bravely, lifting her chin. "Especially since you're the one always worrying about wasting money." She knew she was deliberately baiting him, and she didn't care.

He scooped her into his arms and headed for the sofa, dropping to the seat and putting her facedown over his lap. Before she could comprehend what was happening, he had stripped her jeans and panties to her thighs and trapped her hands at the small of her back.

He bent over her. "Last chance, Lori. Take it back. Or suffer the consequences."

She lay there mute, feeling moisture gather between her thighs.

Without warning a large, flat palm came down hard on her butt. "Ouch!" she cried indignantly.

He spanked her again and again, hard enough to hurt. Badly. Her ass was on fire. But so were other parts of her.

She wriggled in his hold, trying to break free. He subdued her easily, continuing to bring his hand down on her soft, pliable rump with forceful swats. Her sex tingled and throbbed. She squirmed, trying desperately to press her aching clit against his thigh.

Suddenly the spanking stopped. She felt his thumb probe her pussy, and she groaned deep in her chest.

He released her hands and fondled her nipples. She lay across his lap like a rag doll, whimpering weakly while searing pleasure racked her body.

She felt an explosive climax slide ever closer. She whispered his name.

He cursed sharply beneath his breath, tumbled her to the carpet, and bolted from the room. Moments later she heard the front door slam.

Stunned, trembling, she picked herself up and fixed her clothes.

On rubbery legs, she stumbled up the stairs to the guest room, pulled out her two boxes of toys, and began to plan her revenge.

Kent was a mess. He'd spent a sleepless night at a cheap motel out by the interstate. The sound of tractor-trailer rigs pulling in and out all night had kept him awake.

The memory of his wife's hot pink ass kept him stretched on a rack of guilt. He had never before laid a hand on Lori. But she had pushed him to the limit, and he had snapped. Admittedly, she seemed to like it, but that didn't excuse his own violent pleasure in punishing her. Every time he thought about it, he got hard again. God, the vision of it in his head was enough to make him curl up in the fetal position, his aching dick trapped between his legs.

By dawn's first light, he was in the bathroom splashing water on his face and preparing to face the day. He dressed for work, not even bothering to glance in the mirror. He knew he looked like hell. He didn't need any reminders.

By the time he got to the bank he had reached a state of unnatural calm. He couldn't do anything about his erection. It refused to go away for more than fifteen minutes at a time. He kept his suit jacket buttoned, and he remained behind his desk as much as possible.

At ten, his boss stopped by and sat in the chair across from Kent's desk. The pleasant, sandy-haired man was balding and had a paunch. He was also smart as hell and a great administrator.

They exchanged pleasantries for a few moments, and then the chief gave him a smile. "I appreciate all the Saturday hours you've worked, Kent. You've been pulling your weight and then some. People up the line have noticed, not just me."

Kent managed an appropriate smile, but couldn't think of a response.

The boss continued. "It's time somebody else covered the weekend shifts. Why don't you stay here and get your hours in today, and then stay home this Saturday? You deserve it."

Kent panicked. "No." He realized by looking at the other man's face that his shocked negative had been a bit too loud. He cleared his throat. "I mean, thank you, sir, but no, thanks. Not necessary. This schedule I'm working right now suits my family and me just fine. Really. I may eventually want to have a Saturday off here and there, but for now let's keep things like they are."

He held his breath while his superior studied him with a cocked head. Finally, the older man nodded, puzzlement on his face. "Well, okay, then, Davenport. If that's what you want."

"It is," Kent muttered, trying not to sound either desperate or fervent.

When his boss left, Kent slumped back in his seat and waited for his heartbeat to return to normal. It struck him as hilarious that he would have quit his job—simply walked out of the bank and never come back—if he'd had to stay this afternoon.

The clock moved with agonizing slowness, but finally he was able to leave. He debated skipping lunch, but he finally decided he didn't want to waste time on food later, and he really was starving.

He went through the drive-through at the Golden Arches and ordered a burger and fries. He sat in his car and scarfed it down while he watched kids playing on the playground. All around him, the world seemed normal. People laughed. Dogs barked. Mostly bare trees swayed in the wind, signaling the passing of fall and the winter season soon to come.

Nothing anywhere seemed to suggest that today was any different from any other day.

But he knew it was . . . He knew, thank God, that it was finally Tuesday.

He made it home a few minutes earlier than usual. The house looked deserted. Lori must have parked her car in the garage.

He left his Mazda in the driveway and went inside, his heart thumping and his throat tight. He dumped his stuff in the foyer and made himself walk calmly into the kitchen. He got a bottle of water from the fridge, stood quietly, and drank it straight down, his eyes on the clock.

When the bottle was empty, he tossed it in the recycling bin and walked up the stairs. The whole time his ears were straining to hear anything . . . anything at all. But despite his best efforts, he registered nothing but dead silence.

He stumbled on the third step from the top. *Shit.* What if her car wasn't in the garage after all? What if she wasn't even home?

His stomach flipped over once . . . hard . . . and settled into a knot. He gripped the banister, white-knuckled. He wanted to call out her name. To have some reassurance that he wasn't going to be left high and dry while his wife was at the beauty shop. Or the dry cleaner. Or the damned grocery store.

He forced himself to breathe normally. Lori wouldn't do

that. Not today. She'd given him his instructions and he would follow them.

He stripped off his clothes as he strode into the bedroom, dropping them along the way. His shower was brief and, for once lately, not cold. Not today.

He toweled off and rummaged through the dresser, looking for a pair of navy silk boxers Lori had given him for Valentine's Day a year ago. Silk drawers weren't exactly his thing, but he knew she liked them, and he wanted to use every advantage he could muster.

He glanced at the bed. It was neatly made. He pulled back the spread and then the thin blanket and the top sheet, folding them as carefully as he could at the foot of the bed. He replaced the shams against the headboard and propped the pillows against them.

Then, feeling slightly ridiculous, he sat down on the mattress and leaned back. A few seconds later he cursed and sat up to swing his legs over the side of the bed and rest his elbows on his knees. He glanced at the clock on the bedside table. One twenty-seven.

Tension tightened the muscles in his neck and shoulders, and a dull headache pounded in his temples. God, how much longer could he wait?

At a noise behind him, he jerked around and caught his breath. His wife stood in the doorway, a half smile on her lips. If he'd given it much thought, he would have expected to see her appear in pretty, sexy lingerie. But again she surprised him.

She was completely nude. Her long, glorious hair curled at her shoulders, and her lovely breasts were high and firm. Her waist narrowed and then flared into the curve of her hips.

Sometime in the last seven days his unpredictable little wife had found time for a bare-ass-naked bikini wax. He stared at the juncture of her thighs and sighed in appreciation.

She laughed softly and snapped her fingers. "My eyes are up here, Kent."

He refocused his gaze with difficulty. His wife's wry grin was good-natured. He shrugged. "You can't blame a guy for looking."

She stepped into the room, and his temperature spiked. He stood up and faced her, his arms hanging loosely by his sides. "I thought you weren't coming." His relaxed pose was a masterful piece of acting.

She moved closer. Now he could smell her perfume. She had put on more than usual. The sweet, familiar fragrance soothed him.

She smiled gently. "Now, why would you think that? It's Tuesday, isn't it?"

"God, yes," he muttered, wanting to touch her, but afraid to be so bold. Lori had said she would be calling the shots. "I thought this day would never come," he admitted, his throat raw with suppressed emotions. "You succeeded beyond your wildest dreams."

She frowned slightly. "What do you mean?"

He shrugged, prepared to lay his guts on the line. "You made me crave it . . . sex . . . your body. I haven't been able to think about anything else."

A pulse beat in her throat. Her lips trembled, and then she seemed to get control of herself. She swallowed visibly. "That's good," she whispered. "But it's only the beginning. I'm just getting started."

For the first time he noticed the blindfold she held in her right hand. His prick was already at full attention, but it flexed and swelled even more when he pondered the implications of that innocent-seeming prop. It was made of smooth black leather lined with cream-colored lamb's wool.

He was so hard, he hurt. Lori had already sneaked several glances at his cock. He hoped she was a fraction as hungry as he was.

He pointed toward the mask she held. "Shall I put that on you?"

Lori shook her head, a small smile lifting the corners of her mouth. "No. This is for you, Kent. Come here and let's get started."

Chapter Four

Lori watched her husband's face carefully. His reactions were etched there for her to see. Shock. Unease. Arousal. Acquiescence.

He shifted from one foot to the other. His shaft was enormous, or perhaps she had forgotten how impressive it could be. She wanted to fling herself on her knees and gather his cock and balls in her hands, sucking and licking him until he came in her mouth.

Her thighs quivered. She knew she was wet already, and her sex throbbed and ached. She wanted to climax so badly she had to force herself to remember her careful plan. Holding back would be a challenge.

Kent's eyes were wary. "For me?"

She let her gaze slide over him from head to toe. His body language was fierce, even though she could tell he was trying to feign relaxation. Muscles in his chest and arms stood out in relief, and his legs were braced in a fighting stance.

She nodded. "We're going to play a little game of hide-and-seek. I'll hide. You seek. Don't worry: We won't leave this room. And I've moved all the fragile items."

Now he seemed more puzzled than concerned. "And when I catch you?"

She lifted one shoulder. "That's up to you."

His jaw thrust forward. Determination and lust flared in his eyes, making her knees weak. He held out his hand. "Give it to me."

She shook her head. "I'll do it. Come here and kneel in front of me."

He approached her with all the wariness of a man confronting a rabid fox. He knelt as she instructed, his hot gaze now locked on the vee of her thighs.

To be on the safe side, she decided to take a precaution. "Put your hands behind your back."

He obeyed reluctantly. She could see on his face how much he yearned to touch her.

She ran her fingers through his hair, drawing his head forward to rest against her belly. "Good boy," she crooned.

His tongue licked the sensitive skin at her navel. She gasped as heat splintered and crackled in her womb. She took a half step back, and while she still could, she placed the blindfold over his eyes, tugging the straps into place and securing them snugly with the Velcro fasteners. His hair was silky beneath her fingertips.

It was amazing that one simple piece of costume could make a man look so sensual, so erotic, so dangerous. He maintained his subservient position, his head bowed, his hands clasped at his back.

She was shaking. The insides of her thighs were damp. She rubbed her legs together, seeking relief from the gnawing hunger. Forgetting her carefully orchestrated plan, she pushed on the top of his head until he got the hint and sat back on his heels.

She stepped closer. "Eat me, Kent," she demanded huskily.

His hands came up to her hips and she slapped them away. "No touching. Just your tongue."

He groaned and shuddered, but put his hands behind him once again. He pressed closer, and his tongue stabbed against her wet, slick folds. She cried out, shocked by the sharp pleasure engendered by his determined, rhythmic caress.

Every touch of his tongue weakened her knees. In an embarrassingly short time, her world went black and she climaxed forcefully, twisting and grinding her pelvis against his face.

She wanted to collapse in a heap on the rug and let him fill her and fuck her hard, but she shook her head and tried to clear her thoughts. Breathing raggedly, she touched his forehead. "Enough," she whispered as he continued to lap at her juices.

She took his arm. "Stand up."

He obeyed, and she led him to stand in front of the closed bedroom door. She pushed on the back of his head. "Rest your forehead on the door and count to thirty. You can move your arms now. Good luck."

Kent's mouth was dry, his legs shaky. What kind of game was Lori playing . . . besides the obvious? He knew how to go about hide-and-seek. But what did she want from him when he caught her?

He counted to thirty slowly, his mind racing in circles. When he finished, he turned around and rested his back against the door. He knew she hadn't left the room, so this should be easy.

With the blindfold bound snugly around his head, his world was completely dark. He stepped forward carefully and eased his way over to the bed. He went down on his knees and reached under the bed. His hand found nothing but air and one pair of sandals.

He rolled to his feet again and listened intently. A faint sound behind him fueled the adrenaline pumping through his veins. The closet. He moved with a bit more confidence, pausing only once to curse in pain as the corner of the footboard caught his shin.

He held out both hands and found the sliding door to their closet. One side was open. He reached in and rifled amongst the clothes, going all the way to the back wall. Nothing. He bent and probed toward the floor. Still nothing.

He shut that side and slid the opposite door open. A whiff of Lori's perfume teased his nose. He grinned, sure she was hiding there. But a careful search yielded another blank.

Frustration began to build. He'd waited a whole damn week. He wanted her . . . now.

He abandoned the closet and realized with some chagrin that she could be hiding in plain sight up against the wall. He picked a corner and started to make his way around the room, sliding his palms over the wallpaper in careful sweeping motions.

Another faint sound made him freeze. Was she moving from place to place? It was possible. An image of his nude wife tiptoeing around him while he searched like a damned blind man lit the fuse of his anger and notched up his arousal.

His hunting instincts kicked in with a surge of testosterone. He wouldn't let his quarry elude him much longer.

He called out her name. "Give it up, Lori. You know it's only a matter of time. I saw you look at my cock. I know you want it. It's gonna be good, honey. When you feel me between your legs . . . I'm gonna fuck you till you can't walk. I'm so hungry for you, you may never get out of bed."

As he spoke in a low, coaxing voice, he canvassed the room, moving toward the bathroom. Every few minutes he could swear he heard her moving again, probably right under his nose.

Finally she made a mistake. She bumped into something, and he whirled around and grabbed, managing to grope a handful of breast before she giggled and eluded him yet again.

147

His patience wore thin. He heard a tiny thud and he knew she was in the bathroom. He held his hands out, his arms wide, and crossed the room, sweeping the air in regular motions. As his feet came in contact with the cool tile floor, he paused.

The bathtub. He reached forward and jerked the shower curtain aside, making the little steel balls screech along the rod. He slapped toward the back wall, knowing that at any minute he would find her.

But he came up empty, his hands probing uselessly at the far side of the shower enclosure. "Damn it to hell." He growled out his growing frustration.

Suddenly it dawned on him: She could be right beneath him, crouching in the tub. But his insight came too late. A rustle, a brush at his hip, and he knew he was losing her again.

"Not bloody likely." He grabbed with both hands and caught her around the waist just as she tried to slip into the bedroom. Her skin was warm and smooth beneath his hands. He dragged her close and felt her tits crush against his chest.

He thought he heard her moan, but his own urgent lust made him deaf and dumb. He ripped off the blindfold and grabbed a terry-cloth bathrobe from the hook on the wall. He pushed Lori to her knees, tucked the thick fabric beneath her belly, and bent her over the tub.

Her hair fell forward, obscuring her face. Her hands rested in the bottom of the tub. Her ass was the most beautiful thing he had ever seen.

If she said anything, he didn't hear it. All he could think about was getting inside her. He dropped to his knees, the hard tile bruising his bones. He reached between her thighs and probed with two fingers. She was wet and slick and hot as fire.

With shaking hands he positioned his cock and thrust wildly, filling her to the hilt. He felt the beginnings of his orgasm and wanted to weep with angry denial. Not yet, damn it. Not yet. He closed his eyes and gritted his teeth, willing back the tide with superhuman effort. He pinched Lori's ass. "Don't move," he growled. "Not a single muscle."

She went perfectly still, and he ran his hand from her shoulders to her waist. He slid his palms over her sweet ass and gripped her butt cheeks. The urge to move made him breathless.

Seconds passed. Minutes. Maybe aeons. Her vaginal walls gripped him in a tight, relentless sheath. Oh, God, he wanted to move.

By agonizing increments, the imminent explosion banked to a manageable level. He gathered a handful of her hair. "Are you okay?" His husky question reflected the brief shame he felt. He'd practically attacked her.

Her reply was light and teasing. "Am I allowed to move now?"

He chuckled, still damn close to the edge. "I may not be much good to you this go-round. But I'll do better, I promise."

She pushed her bottom back against the cradle of his hips. "Too much talk," she panted. "I liked you better when you were a man of action."

He knew she was deliberately taunting him, but her words stung. "I'll show you action," he muttered.

He withdrew, leaving only the head of his prick to rotate in teasing circles against her labia. Even that stimulation was almost too much. He slid in an inch and back out. Lori whimpered.

He pulled harder on her hair, forcing her head up. "Put your hands on the wall." He ground out the words, feeling a captor's triumph.

She obeyed instantly, the slightly new position giving him a different angle of penetration. He reached beneath her and cupped a breast. "I love your tits," he whispered roughly, his words little more than a guttural slur.

Her inner muscles clenched as he fondled and twisted her sensitive nipples.

She writhed against him. "Kent . . . please."

He laughed hoarsely. "Please what?"

He decided he had enough control to try again. He surged deeper, sweat breaking out on his forehead. *Sweet Jesus.* He'd never felt arousal like this, clawing at his spine, twisting and clenching his gut in painful knots. He panted, sliding his penis out and rubbing it along her butt crack.

He lay forward on her back, nuzzling her neck. "A man should be able to fuck his own wife," he said sullenly, reliving each agonizing night of the last week.

She hissed. "So do it."

"Maybe I won't." In his mind, he saw himself walking away,

leaving her unfulfilled, racked with need. The indignant, ill-used husband cheered the plan. But the horny lover was more practical.

He raked his teeth down her spine. "Who am I kidding?" he said softly. "I couldn't leave this room if the house was burning down around us. I'll die if I don't have you. It's as simple as that."

He lifted her hips a fraction and repositioned his cock. "Beg me, Lori. Give me some satisfaction for the hell you've put me through this week."

He couldn't see her expression, but her words were provocative. "Why should I? I didn't do anything wrong. You're the one who decided sex with me was so unimportant it could be tacked onto your to-do list at the end of the day."

"Beg me."

"Go to hell."

He saw red. Literally. Her flippant response flicked him on his last raw nerve. "That's it. I'm done talking." He entered her with a slam that nearly sent her crashing into the wall.

She braced herself and tried to laugh. "Is that the best you can do?"

He snapped. He went at her like crazy man, thrusting and pounding until he roared and shuddered and emptied himself deep in her pussy, filling her with his hot, sweet come.

In the aftermath, he gathered her in his arms and they collapsed on the hard, cold floor, limbs trembling, bodies shaking.

When he realized she was covered in goose bumps, he scooped

her up and carried her to the bed. He deposited her carefully on the bare sheets, crawled in beside her, and pulled up the covers.

They cuddled, touching and stroking and murmuring silly love words. His chest was tight, and his eyes burned. He smoothed her hair from her face. "Don't you know men hate having to admit it when their wives are right?"

She grinned sleepily, her eyelids drooping, her cheeks flushed. "It should be easy with all the practice you get."

He bit her neck, leaving a mark. "Smart-asses like to live dangerously, don't they?"

She ran a hand up his thigh, and he flinched when she found his dick. His erection hadn't diminished noticeably, despite his recent explosive orgasm.

She raised an eyebrow. "Does this salami thing you call a penis *ever* deflate?"

He shrugged modestly. "Not lately. I've told it to be on high alert." He teased her closest nipple and watched it pucker on cue.

Lori's eyes fluttered shut and she sighed, her thighs moving apart ever so slightly.

He continued his gentle assault on her nipple. "You know, honey, if you weren't taking the pill, I probably would have made you pregnant just then."

She rubbed his balls in lazy circles. "Confident, are we?"

He swallowed and tried to keep the thread of the conversation going when her fingers encircled him. "I was saving up," he reminded her. "Lots of little baby makers reporting for duty."

She opened her eyes, and the love he saw in their smoky moss green depths made his throat ache. "We have plenty of time for that. I'm selfish, Kent. I want you to myself for a while longer."

He flopped back onto the mattress and shivered when the rhythm of her hand picked up. She knew exactly what he liked. But after a long, pleasant moment, he stopped her. "Quit trying to seduce me, woman. You're not the only one with plans."

He rolled out of bed and went to the bathroom to retrieve the blindfold. Lori's eyebrows rose toward her hairline when she saw what he held in his hand.

She shook her head. "I call the shots, remember?" A tiny note of panic in her protest made him grin.

"This is America, babe." He crawled on top of her and straddled her waist, leaning back on his heels. "Everybody gets a vote."

He could see her instinctive refusal written on her face. He paused and waited. "Scared, Lori?"

She licked her lips, her hands covering her breasts in an oddly protective fashion. "No."

"But?"

She looked away, pouting. "I was supposed to be in charge. You agreed."

"You said I could participate," he reminded her gently.

Her lips twisted. "Not like this."

"Be spontaneous, Red. You might like it."

He lifted her head and put on the blindfold, taking care to

keep her hair from being tangled in the straps. The black leather against her white skin made quite a picture.

Her small teeth bit into her bottom lip. He caressed her cheek. "Relax," he said softly. "I'll take care of you."

Her entire body was rigid, and he realized that she felt more vulnerable than he had in a similar position. For him the blindfold had been an annoyance, a barrier between him and what he wanted. But for Lori it was clearly a means of control, of subjugation.

She lay passive and quite obviously apprehensive. That knowledge shouldn't have excited him, but it did. He liked having his wife at his mercy . . . a little too much, if the truth were told.

He studied her for long moments, trying to decide what to do. The possibilities were endless. He lifted her knees so that her feet were flat on the bed. That gave him an unobstructed view of her pretty pink pussy.

He bent and blew softly on her swollen, wet folds. Her hips moved restlessly. With a single fingertip he traced lightly over her clitoris, around and around, up and down. Lori shifted in the bed, her back arching, her breath coming more rapidly.

He left her for a moment and pulled open a drawer in the bedside table. He could use a vibrator, but that was clichéd. Effective, but clichéd nevertheless.

He took out a tube of lubricant, and suddenly his gaze landed on a possibility. Lori adored making love by candlelight, and she had an assortment scattered all over the room. This particular item was a long red taper left over from last Christmas. It was maybe an inch in diameter and seven inches long.

He examined the nonwick end. It was smooth and rounded. He flicked off one small loose patch of wax and smiled. Excellent.

He smeared some gel around the bottom of the candle and seated himself at Lori's hip. Her fingers gripped the sheet in a death hold. He laid a hand, palm flat, on her belly. "You're all tensed up, honey. Surely you trust me?"

"Not really."

The wry sarcasm in her retort made him laugh. "I won't do anything you can't handle, I promise."

Her breasts rose and fell as she gave a ragged sigh. "That's not much comfort."

"Too bad," he said flatly, remembering how she had tormented him a week earlier.

He probed at her asshole with the candle and held her down when she shrieked. The candle slid in easily. He let it go three inches and stopped.

He bent and whispered in her ear. "Tell me what it feels like."

"I don't like it."

"Liar." He brushed her clitoris. As she moaned he pushed the candle another inch.

"Stop." The panic was clear now.

He touched her lips with a fingertip. "Open your mouth."

She did, and he played her with her tongue, stroking it and

rubbing her teeth. "Suck me," he muttered. When her lips closed around the end of his finger, he felt the tug all the way down to his prick. Her tongue was slightly rough, curling around his finger and sucking at him.

He eased the candle deeper and she stopped. "Keep doing it." His command was guttural. He was having a hard time concentrating.

Finally he tugged his hand away. He held the candle still, watching her face. Below the black leather, her lips looked soft and inviting. "Have you ever wondered if you could take two men at once?" he asked softly, rotating the candle gently.

Her mouth fell open in a silent O of alarm. She shook her head rapidly.

He moved between her thighs, keeping the candle in place. "I'm going to take you now, Lori, while he's in your ass. You'll feel both of us."

He entered her slowly. He could feel the rigid candle pressing against his dick. Her vagina felt tighter than before, almost virginal. The steady squeeze on his swollen cock was excruciatingly pleasurable.

He reached behind her and moved the candle in and out. Lori gave a keening cry and tried to elude his penetration. He moved the candle in time with his thrusts. In. Out. Shallow. Deeper.

She was murmuring indecipherable words, her head thrashing from side to side. He used his free hand to tease her clit with his thumb.

She lifted her hips violently, almost dislodging him. "Kent." His name was barely audible, her lips dry, her voice weak.

He released the candle, leaving it to press into the mattress. He stopped moving, watching in awed amusement as his lovely wife hissed and scratched and demanded satisfaction.

He surged deeper, no longer manipulating the candle, but keeping it in place with the pressure of his body. "You're going to come now, angel, with two men deep inside you. Tell me, sweetheart. Tell me what you feel."

"Yes," she whimpered, panting, groaning. "Oh, God, yes." And she cried out and shuddered as he rammed deeper still and pushed her over the edge into oblivion.

His own release soon followed, and he groaned and pulled out, splattering come over her smooth, waxed mound. He slumped beside her, rubbing his cream into her flesh, wanting to mark her indelibly as his.

She whimpered as he removed the candle. He tossed it aside and massaged the tender, swollen flesh between her thighs with firm strokes, being careful to avoid anything but the lightest touch on her supersensitive clitoris. In seconds she peaked again. This time he rolled her onto his chest as she came, and he played with her puckered anus as she shuddered and trembled in his arms.

He was still hard. He lifted her rag doll body and entered her slowly, savoring the welcoming clasp of her sheath. He was able to stroke forever this time, it seemed. He didn't want to stop.

How could he stop? She was back in his arms again after an eternity of cold, lonely nights.

His thighs finally tensed as he felt himself near the end for one last time. Lori slumped limp in his arms, breathing raggedly, her eyes closed. His hands supported her waist.

He ground the base of his cock against her clit and she murmured a protest. "I can't, Kent."

"Yes, angel. Yes." He let go of her waist and found her clit one more time. She reacted violently to the barest touch. "Come on," he urged. "You can do it."

Exhaustion marked her face. He kept up the rhythm he knew she liked. Her inner muscles clenched, and he smiled grimly, holding back. Waiting.

He shifted her against his belly and surged one last time, able at this new angle to penetrate her so deeply she cried out. It was all she needed. With a weak gasp, she rolled into a long, slow orgasm as he gave himself over to one last, draining climax.

They fell asleep instantly, even though the clock beside the bed said it was not yet five o'clock.

Chapter Five

An hour later, Kent groaned and reached for Lori, feeling the pleasant ache in his muscles. He grinned weakly. *Sweet holy hell.* They'd had one awesome afternoon.

He frowned slightly when he realized Lori was missing. He called her name, but she wasn't in the bathroom either. *Strange.*

His stomach rumbled and his brow cleared. She was probably downstairs getting dinner started. If she was as hungry as he was, she'd want some real sustenance before the next round.

He dressed rapidly in jeans and a T-shirt and went barefoot down the stairs to find his wife.

The kitchen was dark. A really nasty feeling crept through his stomach. He searched every corner of the house until he finally ended up in the guest room.

It was as tidy and impersonal as ever, the bed neatly made, the bathroom sparkling clean. But a small pink envelope rested on the vanity counter.

He picked it up, staring incredulously at what was almost certainly bad news.

He carried it downstairs and fixed himself a peanut butter sandwich, staring at the unwelcome note all the while and trying desperately to decide what it could possibly say.

All the usual bad stuff ran through his mind. She wanted a divorce. She needed some time alone. His improved lovemaking was too little, too late. . . . The endless list of possibilities mocked his ignorance.

Without his health-conscious wife there to stop him, he ate a half dozen Oreos, and followed them with a nutritious glass of milk, hoping that the one might cancel out the other.

With the little pink time bomb tucked in his shirt pocket, he wandered into the den and turned on the TV. He flipped channels, staring blankly at the screen.

When his own cowardice became too much to bear, he ripped it open.

Dear Kent,

I love you more than you can possibly know, and you were nothing short of amazing today. I've wanted you so badly this past week, I thought I would go insane. I didn't realize how much I would miss having you in my arms at night. The sex today was off-the-charts wonderful. I'm already hard at work planning for next Tuesday afternoon. Since my self-control is rather "iffy" where you're concerned, I've removed myself from temptation in the meantime. I'll be at Ginny's this week. I've taken the laptop and plenty of projects to keep me busy. I'll keep in touch via e-mail. I could call, but the sound of your voice makes my knees weak, and I need to be strong. Try to concentrate on work, and Tuesday will be here before you know it. The wait will be worth it, I promise.

Your loving and very satisfied wife,
Lori

He stared in dumb silence at his death warrant. Another week? Was she nuts? He'd barely survived the last seven days. *But look what abstinence brought you in the end.* His subconscious took pleasure in reminding him of the afternoon's delights.

A shiver snaked down his spine as he remembered every moment in Technicolor detail. His breathing grew rough, and his cock hardened again, making him want to weep in frustration. He couldn't bear it. Could he? For the prize that was sure to come?

With a self-derisive curse, he flopped full-length on the sofa and unzipped his jeans, freeing his dick for some medicinal therapy. Lori's words rang in his ears. *I want you addicted, Kent. . . . To me . . . To fucking . . . To climaxing. . . .*

Well, she had her wish. He was there.

After forty-eight of the longest, most agonizing hours of his life, he came up with a fairly workable system. He learned exactly how many beers it took to make him fall dead asleep without waking up sick. He learned exactly how much black coffee was necessary to get him dressed and ready for work. And he learned the appropriate ratio of aspirin to coffee and beer.

He ran five miles after work each day. He located and fixed every project on the "honey-do" list . . . from the leaky faucet in the laundry room to the squeaky door hinge on the back porch to the broken pane of glass in the garage window.

He mowed and trimmed the lawn with military precision. He bought groceries for the next two weeks. He rearranged the cabinets and alphabetized the spices.

He rented and watched educational DVDs from the video store . . . open-heart surgery . . . how to build a deck . . . the mating cycle of the cicada.

But he absolutely, under no circumstances, at any time during the day, thought about having naughty, mind-blowing sex with his absent wife.

The nights were another story. He couldn't control his dreams, even with the twin opiates of beer and exhaustion. Again and again he woke up, gasping and drenched in sweat as he relived one erotic fantasy after another.

His prick was so hard every time that he cursed and rolled to his back and jerked off with angry, despairing efficiency.

After four days, he wondered if he should remove Lori's photograph from his wallet and replace it with a picture of his hand. He was addicted to her, all right. And he was sick with longing.

Lori entered her own house on Tuesday morning and felt like a stranger. A delicious smell from the kitchen turned out to be a pork roast and potatoes and carrots in the slow cooker.

The house was immaculate, not a dust bunny or a speck of dirt anywhere. That was odd, because it looked as if Kent had spent a great deal of time working on the yard. While she was gone, he had even cut back the last of the dying bushes and flowering shrubs and piled mulch in neat beds for the winter months.

She glanced at her watch. It was only ten thirty. She estimated that she had about three hours before her husband returned.

In their bathroom she ran a tubful of water and lavishly added her favorite bath oil. She pulled her hair into a knot on top of her head, stepped into the water, and lay back with a sigh. With a new razor, she shaved her legs until they were silky smooth. She touched up other more intimate areas as well.

She stayed there for a long time until the water grew cool, thinking about Kent, about the past week. The last words he had spoken aloud to her were a week ago, a demand that she climax for the third—or was it the fourth?—time. She took in a deep breath and let it out slowly, striving for a state of calm.

They had exchanged e-mails, brief, unimportant notes about household matters. . . . A change in health insurance coming up. What to get his parents for Christmas. How the neighbor's house had gone up for sale. All of it pleasant . . . cordial.

She hadn't taken her new boxes of sex toys with her when she left. But she'd memorized the contents, and she knew what she would need this afternoon.

She dried off and slipped into a robe before going to the guest room closet and retrieving her new playthings. Carefully she selected the items she had thought about all week.

Lastly she dressed in the pretty black costume. It was basically a tank-style swimsuit covered with high-quality, soft-as-a-whisper feathers. At noon she put it on and looked in the mirror. The front and back plunged in deep vees, putting her cleavage on display and revealing the line of her spine all the way down to her butt.

Snaps between the legs made it possible for an easy exit. It looked okay with her bare feet, but she rummaged in her closet and pulled out a pair of black patent leather high heels she had worn to a wedding in the spring. The four-inch stilettos made her almost as tall as Kent, especially when he was nude.

She sprayed perfume in various warm spots and checked her makeup. She had used a heavy hand with mascara, and her ruby lips were applied with one of those eight-hour lipsticks that wouldn't rub off. She slicked over her mouth with a clear, shiny gloss that made the crimson even deeper.

Everything else she needed was tucked in a towel beneath her side of the bed.

At five after one she heard the front door open. She escaped into the guest room and waited for Kent to take his shower.

Kent followed the same routine as the week before, only this time he was preternaturally calm. He didn't wonder if she would show up, and he didn't dither over what to wear or where to sit. On the way home he had pulled to the side of the road and jerked off in his hand, so his dick was actually hanging in placid, limp contentment for the moment.

After his *warm* shower, he actually took five extra minutes and shaved his face, wanting to be smooth and fresh for his lover. His hand trembled for a brief second as his thoughts strayed to the hours ahead, but he jerked them back and finished his ablutions.

He didn't fool with the boxers this time. He sprawled nude on the bed, his back resting comfortably against the headboard.

But the entire pretense came crashing down around his ears when he heard her footsteps in the hall. Every nerve ending in his body went haywire, and hyperventilation was a real threat. When she appeared in the doorway, his jaw dropped in stunned disbelief.

His John Thomas reacted instantly, bringing the troops to attention with record speed.

"Lori." The word came out more like a prayer than a greeting.

It hurt to look at her. The sensuality in her stance, the erotic invitation in her smile almost blinded him. For a brief second he thought about pleading for the fleece-lined mask.

Instead he cleared his throat. "You're back."

As a conversational gambit it fell somewhere between stupid and pathetic.

Her smile faded, and it seemed to his already overstimulated brain that she was nervous.

Her lips twisted. "Yes. Did you miss me?"

"You have no idea," he said, unable to completely disguise the ache in his voice.

She touched her breast almost absently, lightly stroking a feather. "I missed you, too."

Was she going to stand there in the doorway forever? The subtle, mesmerizing motion of her hand was hypnotic. He tried to decide if he should go to her, but she seemed like a mystical creature with her own agenda. He was afraid of appearing clumsy or foolish in front of such a goddess.

So he stayed where he was.

Finally she moved toward him. He noticed that her hands were empty this week. She stopped beside the bed and looked down at him, her quiet, somber gaze assessing his obvious arousal.

She cocked her head. "Will you close your eyes and not peek?"

He nodded jerkily and complied. He heard a rustle and some clinking noises and smelled a pleasant scent, maybe almond or something similar.

He felt her take his arm and stretch it toward the headboard. His eyes flew open in spite of his promise, just in time to see her secure his wrist to the bed with sturdy leather restraints.

"Lori . . ." His quickly curtailed protest was urgent.

She ignored him and crossed to the other side of the bed, repeating the process with his left wrist.

While he watched, aghast, she secured his ankles as well. He could have struggled, but he didn't. And he wasn't sure why. Because he sure as hell had a bad feeling about this.

She bent over beside the bed, and he realized that she had some kind of erotic stash tucked away.

Moments later a small ceramic pot appeared on the nightstand. Its hot scented oil filled the room with heavy fragrance. It was the aroma he had recognized in the beginning, only stronger now that it was burning.

She paused in her preparations and glanced at him with a frown. "I asked you to close your eyes."

He did so reluctantly, straining to hear. He felt her hand brush his chest, and without warning a searing pain stabbed into his right nipple. He gasped and flinched as the hot, sharp bite sent shards of fire through every nerve center in his body.

He was almost prepared when the second nipple was assaulted. Almost, but not quite. He shuddered and barely managed to suppress a groan.

"You may look now." Her quiet voice held a note of authority.

He blinked and tried to peer at his chest. Two small brass

nipple clamps lined in velvet were attached lewdly to his chest. He swallowed hard, remembering with sickening clarity an occasion when he had mentioned wanting to try such a thing.

He'd watch his stupid mouth in the future.

She studied him almost dispassionately, gauging his discomfort. "Can you bear it?"

He heard the doubt in her voice, and that stupid, self-defeating masculine pride jumped into the fray. "Of course," he lied, his brief, terse response just shy of insolence.

She nodded once. "Good."

She glanced at his cock. The immediate agony had wilted his eagerness for a moment, but somehow, now that the pain had dulled to a burning ache, his traitorous prick was indicating approval.

She picked up a plastic bowl and put it on the mattress beside his hip. She frowned. "I need you to get rid of that erection for this next part."

Those words were almost enough to make him shrivel, but a week's wait, even given the multitudinous hand jobs, kept him firm. She used a washcloth to pick up two large ice cubes. Ignoring his choked protest, she began icing down his balls.

At first the sensation was pleasurable, but soon the biting cold began to do its work. Even with her hands on him, the discomfort was enough to make him go limp.

When his penis lay soft and flaccid against his thigh, she

reached beside the bed again and picked up a cock ring. He had seen them only in pictures, but he knew what they were for.

Anxiety flared. "Um, Lori . . ."

She bent over him, her brow creased in concentration. "Don't worry," she said with the blithe disregard of someone who couldn't possibly understand a male's innate caution in such situations. "The catalog said this adjustable kind is okay for beginners. It won't damage anything, I promise."

"Let's hope not," he grumbled.

She lifted his balls gently and slid them though the metal circle. Actually it was two metal semicircles joined by narrow leather, hence the adjustable component. When she had his balls the way she wanted them, she tucked his shaft through and tightened the fastener.

She tugged firmly, watching his face. "Is that comfortable?"

He shrugged, not sure what to tell her. The constriction was snug, but not painful. "I guess so. It doesn't hurt, if that's what you're asking." Not like the nipple clamps that felt like hot pokers in his chest.

She nodded, satisfied. "Good."

She leaned down one last time and picked up her digital camera.

"Now wait a damn minute." He jerked and twisted, frantic, vulnerable, embarrassed. The more he flailed, the more his prick grew. While Lori snapped picture after picture, he lay helpless as a baby.

The ring around his cock and balls definitely seemed tighter now. The hot ache in his prick was unlike anything he had ever experienced. He felt harder, fuller . . . hell, even longer.

Finally Lori put down the camera. She touched one of the nipple rings. "You look good like this," she murmured, her gaze sweeping him from head to toe.

The arousal that rolled through his veins was seductive and oxygen-stealing. He was having trouble breathing, and his chest was tight. He wanted to hold her down and fuck her . . . but he didn't want to give up the drugging mix of sensations that kept him hovering on a precipice of urgent need.

She walked to the dresser and pressed a button on the small boom box they kept there to listen to news and weather while they got ready in the mornings. Now, instead of talk radio, music filled the room. It sounded Greek, or maybe Middle Eastern.

While he watched, Lori lifted her arms above her head and began to sway. He knew she was talented and graceful, but she had never danced just for him. He watched, mesmerized, as she bent and turned, her hips and legs moving rhythmically to the heavy, throbbing beat.

He began to feel the haunting music in his dick, in his burning nipples. The cock ring tightened. Blood pulsed in his engorged cock, making him groan and move restlessly in his restraints.

By the time the music faded away, he was almost frantic. "Lori, please, baby. Let me go. I can't stand it. I've got to have you."

She tugged at her bodice and extracted a single black feather. "You'll have me."

Her husky promise did nothing to calm him, because the look in her eyes promised more sensual games. She came back to the bed and sprawled beside him, her head on his chest, carefully avoiding his nipples.

She held the feather above his groin and chuckled. "I can't let you go yet. We're just getting started."

She brushed the feather over his balls and he cursed fervently, trying in vain to evade her delicate torture. The sensation of the feather on his testicles was hard to explain—rather like slender, fiery string marking his skin with an invisible brand.

He was ready to beg for mercy when she finally desisted. While his chest heaved with frantic breaths, she touched his crotch. She examined his cock and balls with light, fleeting touches. The ring bit into his flesh, producing a dark, almost frightening pleasure.

She kissed the swollen head of his penis, swirling her tongue around his shaft and licking daintily at the weeping slit. He lifted his hips, begging silently for the hot suction of her mouth.

She ignored his mute plea.

She stood up again, rubbing her hands over the silky black feathers that framed her fresh, sensual beauty. "Do you like this?" she asked, her eyes dark with a mix of indecipherable emotions.

"Your costume?"

"Yes."

"It's beautiful," he said quietly, "but not as lovely as you."

She bent gracefully and released the fastenings between her legs, slipping her fingers into the opening and caressing herself. "It's hot," she admitted.

"Then take it off."

She smiled. "It was expensive."

"Who the hell cares?"

She stripped off the provocative costume and stepped out of it. His first sight of her nude body hit him like a punch to the chest. He stared avidly, hungrily. Had her body been this perfect last week?

She seemed to him at that moment the epitome of female beauty. Again he urged her to release him.

She gathered her hair into a ponytail and tied it back. "Patience, Kent," she taunted, clearly enjoying his frustrated demands.

She approached the bed, and his heartbeat slowed to a measured thud. *Finally.*

With a graceful move that took him totally by surprise, she straddled his waist. Her pussy rubbed deliberately over his erection, making him shudder and curse.

She lifted to her knees and lowered herself onto his cock, wringing an agonized shout from his throat. "The ring, damn it. Take the ring off."

She slid up and down, reaching behind her and gently

squeezing his balls. "No. Just relax. It's supposed to make your orgasm stronger, more intense, prolonged."

That was what he was afraid of. He wasn't sure how much more of this dark, addictive pleasure he could stand. And the thought of shooting off with that damned ring binding him scared him spitless. What if the thing crippled him at a crucial moment?

But he couldn't tell her that. He shook his head, feeling fatalistic. It would either kill him or make him a sexual stud. A hell of a choice.

He tried one more time. "Let me make love to you, honey. Please."

Her smile was wicked. "This is my show. Just close your eyes and come along for the ride."

She abandoned him for a moment and turned around, giving him a dizzying view of her heart-shaped ass. She mounted him again and began to fuck him that way, leaning forward and grasping his legs just below his knees.

Every time she lifted up on his cock, he got a glimpse of her slick, moist folds. Every time she ground down on his prick, he got a glimpse of heaven.

He tried to move, tried to lift into her rhythm. His penis ached and throbbed. He felt his release bearing down, but it seemed just out of reach.

His painful nipples sent trembling messages to his pelvis. His wrists hurt. His legs quivered. He wanted to stroke Lori's ass, play with her pussy, reach around her and cup her breasts, make her come.

But Lori seemed to be doing just fine on her own. She hesitated, up on one knee, fondling her own swollen flesh, and then one last time she pressed down, triggering her climax. He watched, helpless, as she trembled and collapsed on his legs.

Unfortunately, he hadn't been able to join her.

She scooted off of him, and her eyes widened. His cock was thick and red and angry-looking. "Don't move," she whispered.

She disappeared into the bathroom and returned with a warm, damp washcloth. She cleansed him carefully, driving his excitement even higher.

He had never been this aroused without ejaculating.

She tossed the rag aside and took him in her hands. "Now let's finish this," she muttered. Her lips closed around him, and his vision went black.

A guttural moan escaped his throat, and he would have whimpered if it hadn't been unmanly. Every inch of his skin prickled with raw heat that funneled and concentrated in his prick. For a panicked moment he was afraid the shining peak would elude him. The ring around his sex frustrated and infuriated him.

He panted in shallow breaths and concentrated on the feel of Lori's lips, her teeth, her tongue. At last the wave gathered power. He shuddered and twisted and cried out in shocked wonder as his climax bore down and carried him to a place he had never reached before.

His last conscious thought was of Lori. If she was gone when this was over, he wouldn't be responsible for his actions.

But his fears were in vain. When he was coherent again, he turned his head and saw her sitting there, her big green eyes filled with concern.

She touched his hip. "Did it hurt you?"

He laughed hoarsely. "God, yes. In the best possible way. It was incredible. No," he said, instantly correcting himself. "You were incredible."

Amazingly, she blushed. When she removed the first nipple clamp, he yelled like a little girl, cursing as feeling returned with a vengeance, making his earlier discomfort seem like nothing.

Lori, her solemn face anxious, licked his abused flesh, soothing it with soft, wet passes of her tongue. She touched his cheek. "Hold on." Without warning she released the remaining clip.

This time he swallowed his instinctive groan and concentrated on riding out the pain. His wife's delicate tongue caress went a long way toward healing his discomfort.

She glanced down at his still semierect penis. "I don't know if we can get it off yet," she said softly, her gaze worried.

"Untie me, Lori."

This time she obeyed, quickly releasing all four of his limbs. She started to speak, but he tumbled her to her back, spread her legs, and entered her with a quick thrust. From this angle the damned ring felt even tighter. "We'll just have to keep fucking, I guess." He powered them both to another almost simultaneous peak, and slumped, exhausted, onto her soft, welcoming body.

He chuckled weakly. "I don't know if I can keep up with you, sweetheart."

"Vitamins," she said solemnly. "I ordered some special ones just for men."

He laughed until tears trickled down his face. "Why am I not surprised?" He tugged her into a sitting position, giving her his best intimidating stare, not that she seemed particularly impressed. "No more seven-day abstinence tests. I can't take it."

"Me either," she admitted, curling into his embrace. "I want to be with you every night."

"And on Tuesday afternoons?"

"Especially then," she said, tugging at the ring that still bound the family jewels. "I have a lot more plans, as long as you're willing."

He sighed, feeling magnanimous in the wake of more pleasure than any man could expect in one day. "I'm here for you, Lori. Tuesdays and any other day or night you care to name."

And for once, neither of them gave a thought to the future. But they spent the rest of the night in each other's arms, content to explore the amazing present.

G MARKS
THE SPOT

Chapter One

Dani Shapelli loved storms. This one was all fire and fury. She stood at the plate-glass window and watched as ragged lightning strikes rent the sky and lit up the room where she hovered.

It was twilight, that pensive, melancholy moment when day was fading and evening was not yet realized. She put her blue mood down to hormones and her new husband's absence. This was the first time they had spent a night apart.

She sighed, wincing momentarily as a thundering boom shook the house. Trevor traveled frequently. She'd known that when she married him. In fact, they had met at a business conference. For her it had been love at first sight.

Trevor Shapelli was a fascinating man. His father was Italian and his mother English, hence his unusual name. He carried himself with a natural arrogance born of centuries of breeding. On his paternal side, the blood of Roman conquerors ran through his veins. Via his mother's ancestry, he was related to kings and queens.

He was as handsome as he was sophisticated. Jet-black hair and eyes to match combined with an aquiline nose and a strong chin to create a look of almost haughty confidence. But though he was a predator in the business world, he was a kind and loving husband.

From their first flirtatious conversation, he had treated Dani with nothing but respect and admiration. Even so, she'd been a bit intimidated by him in the beginning. Not that she was shy by any means, but he was a decade older than she was, and worlds ahead of her in every kind of experience.

His eyes held a weariness, a fatigue with life in general. But with her that ennui faded, and his face sparkled with humor and enjoyment. He relaxed when they were alone, and the real man behind the public persona appeared.

They'd been married for only eight months. Early on, they had decided to start a family sooner rather than later. Trevor was financially secure, and Dani, just a year shy of thirty, was eager to become a mother. To their delight, she had conceived quickly, but just as quickly she miscarried.

Despite the doctor's reassurances and all the statistics, Dani had been devastated. The experience had made her so upset that they had decided to wait a bit before trying again.

Another violent flash of light drew her attention back to the window. There was no perceptible pause before the crack of thunder followed. The house, built firmly on Oregon bedrock, stood on a windswept cliff overlooking the Pacific Ocean. Far below, angry waves crashed on jagged boulders. It was a wild, romantic scene, and she felt its stormy majesty in her bones.

She wrapped her arms around her waist and yearned for Trevor's quiet, steady strength. Though she had never minded being single, she experienced in his arms a contentment that was life-altering. She was grounded now, in a way she had never been before.

After the miscarriage and her subsequent grief, Trevor urged her to quit work and stay home if that was her wish. She had enjoyed her job, but it was high-stress, and she jumped at the chance to rest and concentrate on her health before trying again to get pregnant.

After six or eight weeks, her emotions stabilized and she began once again to look forward to building a nest for her one-day-to-be family of three. Trevor indulged her shamefully. They planned the nursery together, and he refused to settle for second-best. When the time came, the newest little Shapelli would have the finest Danish crib, the softest Irish linens, all the latest in American ingenuity.

Already the spacious room across the hall from their suite

was a child's fantasy. Fairy sprites adorned the walls, and forest animals peeked out from behind fir trees and fanciful clouds. Trevor was not in favor of knowing the sex of the baby ahead of time, even with required ultrasounds, and Dani agreed. So their plans avoided the usual pinks and blues and instead encompassed a decor that would be suitable for any child.

She pressed a hand to her flat abdomen. She wanted a baby so badly, she was afraid she might be jinxing the process. In odd moments of anxiety she worried that there might be something wrong with her body.

Intellectually she knew it was ridiculous. She had conceived easily, and miscarriages were common. But still the fear lingered.

Trevor was amazing. She knew he had also been deeply disappointed when the pregnancy ended, but he had never wavered in his positive support. He'd pampered her and spoiled her and reminded her often of what a wonderful mother he knew she would be.

So her shaky emotional state had healed, for the most part, and now they were merely waiting a bit to make sure they were ready for the mental stress of trying again after such a heartbreaking loss.

Overall, her health was the best it had ever been. She slept well every night—but that was perhaps because her virile husband made love to her constantly. He was experienced, inventive, and passionate. One moment he made her feel like a cherished goddess, the next a sensual, earthy woman. He knew things about a woman's body that made him dangerously good in bed.

He had bewitched her, lured her deeper into her own sexuality, made her crave his touch. To say she enjoyed their lovemaking was a vast understatement. She shivered, remembering the responses Trevor demanded of her body. Facing their bed tonight . . . alone . . . was not a pleasant thought.

Staying in the house by herself didn't scare her. Although her new home was close to twenty thousand square feet and filled with odd little nooks and crannies, Trevor had installed a state-of-the-art security system, and she felt perfectly safe. She wasn't afraid of the dark.

But she was a bit afraid of how much she loved Trevor. Sometimes the depth of the emotion was overwhelming. In rare moments she questioned the speed of their courtship and marriage. How well did she really know her enigmatic husband?

Everyone had a past, though hers was remarkably boring. But Trevor seemed to have more secrets than most. Take this house, for instance. Why on earth did a single man need this much space? When she pressed him about it, he said he didn't like to feel crowded. That was probably true, but was it the whole story?

The sprawling mansion on the solitary hilltop had a personality all its own. Built in the early 1900s by a wealthy railroad magnate, it was both rambling and mysterious. Most of the original house remained intact, but subsequent owners had remodeled, added on, and redecorated. The resulting ambience was part *Wuthering Heights* and part *The Great Gatsby*.

She had explored many of the rooms, but it would take much longer to know the house in its entirety, every closet and cubby. So far it didn't really feel much like home, but she was trying.

The nursery was almost complete, and now that it was nearly finished, she wondered if she had been hasty in giving up her job. An older woman and her daughter from the nearby town came in to clean once a week, so that left very little manual labor with which Dani could occupy herself.

Tonight, watching the changing moods of the ocean as the storm peaked and swirled, she wished fervently that she had a project to keep her busy. She wasn't much for television, and Trevor's expensive home entertainment center baffled her. She probably could figure out the DVD player in a pinch, but the thought of watching a movie by herself bored her.

Something about the magnificent storm filled the house with an urgent sexual energy. Her breasts tingled and her thighs trembled. She felt like an aching, empty vessel yearning to be filled.

She had already spoken with Trevor earlier. He was in Europe, and with the time difference he'd be sleeping now. Even that made her weepy. She felt so alone. Not lonely, but chilled and isolated. Shut off from the love and laughter that Trevor had brought to her life.

She waited for the last of the storm to fade away into the distance and then went to their bathroom and filled the giant marble tub with water and bath crystals. The evocative scent of magnolia blossoms soon filled the air. She and Trevor had spent part of their honeymoon in Savannah, and he had bought her an entire set of spa products in her favorite fragrance.

She undressed and slipped into the water with a sigh of pleasure. She'd been a bit tense all day, and the warm, silky water soothed and comforted her. She stretched full-length on the built-in seat and lifted her chest until her breasts popped up above the surface of the water. She could feel the hot, swirling bubbles tease her sensitive sex. Her thighs clenched.

In the mirror on the wall along the tub she could see herself in detail. When she first married Trevor, that mirror had made her self-conscious. But he soon cured her of that. He'd fucked her repeatedly, in various positions, making her watch their reflection, refusing to let her close her eyes.

As her shyness faded over time, her appreciation grew for the sensual tableau. Watching Trevor's big, wet hands on her damp, rosy skin made her tremble, even now, after eight months of marriage.

She closed her eyes and imagined his long fingers spreading her thighs, his thick erection nudging her core, pushing insistently until her flesh yielded and he took her deeply. Her head fell back on the hard edge of the tub, wetting her hair. She fingered herself, playing with her swollen clitoris, moaning as the pleasure built and crested.

She drifted lazily in the aftermath, wishing she were not alone.

When the water cooled, she stepped out and dried off. In the vanity mirror opposite the tub, she examined her reflection. Her straight black hair was surprisingly similar in color to her husband's. No blond-headed babies for them.

She stroked over her breasts, down her tummy, to her hips. How would she look when she was several months pregnant? Would her husband still find her attractive? She supposed most women worried about such things.

She couldn't imagine giving up sex, even when she was large and ungainly. Trevor was a man with strong appetites. He would find a way for them to be intimate . . . she had no doubt.

She dressed in her favorite smoke gray silk peignoir set. Trevor had given it to her as an engagement gift, noting with pleasure that it matched her eyes. He had bought it in Paris, and the delicate garments were the loveliest things she had ever owned.

Her orgasm hadn't satisfied her. It was getting quite late, but she still felt restless, too wired to sleep. She rummaged in a box deep in the closet and pulled out her vibrator. The toy had not seen much use since Trevor came into her life.

She drew back the covers on the big, comfy bed and settled against a pile of pillows. She drew her gown and robe to her waist and turned on her plastic friend. Just as she moved the tip toward her aching pussy, the phone rang, startling her and making her heart pound with anxiety.

She grabbed up the receiver. "Hello?"

Trevor's husky voice came through as clearly as if he were in the next room. "It's me, Dani."

She glanced at the clock. "You're awake already?" He sounded drowsy.

"I couldn't sleep. Might as well get up and start the day."

"I hope you're not pushing yourself too hard," she fretted. "You're not immune to jet lag, even if you do think you're Superman."

He chuckled wearily. "I'll rest this afternoon, I promise. I just wanted to hear your voice."

"I miss you," she whispered.

A long silence from his end, and then hoarse words. "I can't believe I left you. I've never hated any trip as badly as this one."

"When will you be back?" She knew he had an open-ended plane ticket because of the fluid nature of his schedule.

"In two days."

"What if you can't get everything done?"

"I'm coming home anyway." His voice was terse . . . frustrated.

"Do what you have to do, Trevor. I'm not going anywhere," she teased softly.

He cursed beneath his breath. "Tell me what you're wearing," he said urgently.

She frowned in confusion. "The Paris negligee."

He groaned. "God, you look amazing in that . . . or out of

it." She could hear the wicked smile in his voice, and her nipples tightened in response.

She took a breath. "Don't you want to know what I'm doing?"

"I assumed you were getting ready for bed."

"I was getting ready for *something*."

His end of the conversation was quiet for about fifteen seconds. "Are you trying to make me crazy?"

"Is it working?" she asked softly, pressing the vibrator between her legs.

His voice sharpened in suspicion. "What's that noise, Dani?"

She sighed as her moist folds felt the hum of the mechanical toy. "My vibrator," she said simply, tucking the phone between her shoulder and her ear for a brief moment and using her free hand to push her hair from her face.

Trevor let forth an impressive string of curses, starting in English and then switching to a heated spate of Italian. "Tell me," he demanded. "Tell me what you're doing."

She pouted, even though he couldn't see her. "You're awfully bossy." The vibrator was doing its job, and with that combined with her husband's voice, she was feeling the effects rather quickly.

"Please, sweetheart." His hoarse plea made her shiver.

She pressed inside her pussy, stroking herself deeply. She couldn't quite suppress the gasp as she hit a sweet spot. "I'm screwing myself with it," she admitted, her voice soft and languid.

"Oh, God, Trevor. I wish you were here. I love it when you suck my nipples."

"Shit." His choked response made her curious.

"Trevor? Are you touching yourself?" Imagining his big hands on his own prick sent her arousal surging upward several notches.

His word was tight: "Yes."

Her head fell back against the pillows, the phone pressed to her ear. She withdrew the vibrator and began sliding it gently over and around her clitoris. Her thighs trembled. "I love your cock," she whispered. "I'm imagining you entering me right now."

He was breathing heavily. "I'll go deep, baby. You'll feel me all over your body."

She licked her lips. "Is your cock really hard?"

"As granite."

"Will you spread my legs?"

"As wide as they'll go."

"Will it stretch me when you slide in?"

"Yeah . . . a lot."

She lost the thread of the conversation as her orgasm began to bear down on her. Her breathing was jerky. The vibrator plunged deep again. "Trevor . . ." His name was a keening cry. She bent her knees and lifted her hips off the bed as she climaxed. Her vagina clamped around the vibrator and pulsed with ripple after ripple of satisfaction.

She dropped the phone at one point and had to retrieve it. She closed her eyes and snuggled deeper into the pillows. "Trevor?"

"What, angel?"

"I came."

The smile in his voice was impossible to miss. "Yeah, I noticed."

Now that she no longer held the vibrator, her free hand played with her aching nipples. "And you?"

"Not yet." His voice was husky. "Talk me through it."

She smiled. "If I were there with you, I'd have you in my mouth already."

A muffled word from his end.

She pinched her nipples one at a time, feeling moisture gather again between her legs. "I'd suck hard," she whispered. "Making you even harder. And then I'd straddle your lap and feel you shove up inside me, filling me, probing deep."

She wondered if he was still able to hold the phone, but she kept talking. "Every time you stroke in and out, I shiver. I want to keep you inside me all night, fucking and fucking until we fall asleep exhausted." She paused and listened.

A shuddering groan from Trevor assured her he was nearing the end.

She lowered her voice to a husky promise. "And then, when you are absolutely sated, I'll take you in my mouth and lick you and eat you until you stretch my lips again, swelling and thickening until you explode."

A muffled shout, and then her name . . . in an anguished cry.

She felt his climax as if it were her own. And she ached. "Trevor?"

Finally he spoke. He sounded exhausted but somewhat appeased. "I'm here, Dani. That barely scratched the surface, you know."

She smiled. "Perhaps we can try again later today. If you have time."

"I'll make time," he muttered.

She yawned and slid beneath the covers. She hated to hang up, but exhaustion suddenly overwhelmed her.

Trevor made it easy. "Go to sleep, Dani. Dream of us. And when you wake up, we'll . . . talk again."

She nodded, feeling her eyelids droop. "I love you, Trevor."

"I love you, too."

Trevor hung up the phone and stood, stretching nude in the cool morning air. He was in Milan, and the sparkling morning light lifted his spirits, despite his hunger for his wife.

He threw back the shutters and inhaled deeply, feeling the blood surging through his veins. He had always loved the constant stimulation of travel. But never before had home been a draw. Never before had he left a part of himself behind.

He reached for his flaccid prick and massaged it absently, thinking of his beautiful wife. Oddly enough, she was not at all the type of woman he had been attracted to in the past. He'd been with many women. Too many, probably. But he loved the female body with a passion, particularly lush breasts and plump, curvy asses.

Dani was nothing at all like the women he usually found himself pursuing. But he'd known her for less than a half hour when he decided he had to have her. She was a slip of a woman, slight and almost flat-chested. She was lithe and graceful, and her quicksilver charm captivated him from the moment they met. The first time he heard her lilting, happy laugh, he felt a giant fist squeeze his chest.

He'd courted her and married her without delay, fearful that some other man would steal her away. He knew his uneasiness was unfounded. He had only to look in Dani's eyes to see her devotion to him.

Her sharp intelligence, gentle humor, and unflagging zest for life warmed his heart in a way no woman ever had. He was head over heels in love with his new wife.

Although she was not all that experienced in the bedroom, she was wise beyond her years about life. Already she had taught him so much about love and contentment. At one time he had used his enormous house to hide away from the world. He could be moody and sullen on occasion. But with Dani in his life, he found himself imagining that huge house filled with children and laughter.

He wanted to be with her now.

Thinking of Dani in their bed, aching, ready for sexual release, made him hard again.

He looked down into the piazza below and saw a nameless signorina going about her daily chores. Her long fall of raven's-wing hair looked much like his wife's, and she had the same little spring in her step.

He closed his eyes and leaned against the window frame, pulling urgently at his cock. He felt the sunshine on his bare skin, warming his turgid penis from without, even as images of his nude wife stoked the heat from within. He was not an exhibitionist, but he couldn't bring himself to back away from the open window.

The vibrance of the new day fed his arousal, making him feel achingly alive. He picked up the familiar rhythm, squeezing and stroking, wanting desperately to turn and find his love sprawled across the feather mattress behind him.

He imagined it so. In his dreams he went to her and lifted her buttocks in his palms, resting her legs on his shoulders. From this position he could enter her deeply, thrusting hard against her womb. He heard her cry out, felt the excitement in her voice and her pulsing core. With sweat on his forehead, he deliberately slowed his thrusts, taunting them both.

Dani struggled in his grasp, trying to force him to completion. He held her immobile, feeling his seed rise inexorably. He laughed when she cursed him.

He looked at her small, rounded tits, her dewy skin, her rosy lips. He trembled, feeling his climax hovering in the wings. Finally he pushed forward again, wringing a gasp from her throat. Her inner muscles caressed him, making his head spin.

He pumped slowly, trying to savor every second of shivering pleasure. But the wanting was too intense, the hunger too severe. With hand and mind, he pumped his way to a barely satisfying orgasm, crying inwardly for the emptiness of the release.

He stumbled into the bathroom, breathing jerkily. He turned on the shower and stepped beneath the hot, revitalizing spray.

He couldn't seem to sate the beast that prowled within him. Even as he soaped his torso and his arms and legs, his thoughts strayed as he imagined Dani in his embrace. Their shower stall at home was decadent in size and amenities. He thought of the time he had used the shower massage head to tease her pussy. He remembered her gasping pleasure, the faint look of shock on her face as she climaxed with no more than the focused stream of water for stimulation. He soaped his own cock, imagining her fingers on his shaft. The slippery feel of his hand on his firm flesh made him tremble and growl with frustration.

He rinsed off and dried himself, wincing as the towel abraded his sensitive nipples and groin.

In the bedroom he sprawled on the mattress again, closing his eyes and reaching for a memory to keep him warm. The night before he left, Dani had been amazing. She had begun that evening by giving him a surprisingly expert massage. Her fingers burrowing into his taut muscles had been both relaxing and arousing. And that odd dichotomy made him weak with hunger.

She started her therapy with him facedown, but when she offered to complete the session by working on his front, he snapped, startled by his own loss of control. He pushed her to her back and literally pinned her to the floor, hammering into her cunt with pistonlike force. He knew she reached a climax. She told him so later. But in that moment of near insanity, he'd been conscious of nothing but the searing need to spill his come inside her body and never let her go.

The knowledge that he was leaving the following day was no doubt the trigger for his caveman behavior. That and the fear that she would not feel the pain of their separation half as much as he did.

He'd wanted her to remember that last fuck. Wanted her to ache for him as deeply as he did for her.

The swelling of his cock was almost painful. He gripped it in a firm grasp and moved his hand in quick, jerky motions. With a groan that ripped from his nuts up his spine to his throat, he shot off for the third time, breathing heavily and calling her name in vain.

Chapter Two

Dani slept fitfully, haunted by erotic dreams. In her subconscious, the storm never abated. It continued to rumble and roar, building in intensity, even as the hunger in her body rose to new heights.

She awoke sometime around four a.m., drenched in sweat from the covers she had piled around her. She whimpered as shards of heat pulsed between her legs. She'd become dependent on Trevor's sensual attentions already, and without him to warm her bed, she was frustrated and petulant.

She used her hand one last time to find momentary relief, and finally fell into a deep sleep.

✳   ✳   ✳

When she awoke it was midmorning. Her head throbbed from staying in bed too long. She stumbled downstairs and gulped down her first cup of coffee.

In stark contrast to yesterday's stormy weather, this morning had dawned with blue skies and fluffy white clouds. The brilliant light hurt her eyes, and the placid clouds mocked her turbulent thoughts.

The house was eerily quiet. She couldn't face breakfast. Instead, she dressed in jeans and a T-shirt and her most comfortable pair of sneakers. Now that she was married to Trevor, even her casual clothes carried designer labels, but today she purposely dressed like the old Dani. She planned to snoop, and that meant, by default, being disloyal to Trevor.

Not that she intended any harm. He had told her again and again that this was her house now, as well as his. He'd given her carte blanche to strip it down to the bare walls and start over if she wanted to.

But she rather liked the old house the way it was. She had no plans to change much of anything. But she did want to explore. And today seemed like the perfect opportunity.

The cleaning ladies were not paid to give attention to the third floor. In fact, the door at the top of the stairwell was locked. Dani had a key. Trevor had made sure she had a full set of keys and alarm codes for every section of the house.

She retrieved her key ring and noted the careful markings on each individual key. Trevor was detailed and meticulous, and she had no trouble finding the one she wanted.

She climbed the steep stairs with faint trepidation, wondering why she was allowing the indisputable aura of musty, gloomy days gone by to weigh so heavily on her mood. Surely she wasn't so fainthearted that a few possible ghosts worried her?

The thick oak door opened with a mighty creak when she inserted the key in the lock and turned it. She found the light switch and flipped it on. Antique wall fixtures intended to simulate gas lamps emitted a subdued glow. The floor plan on this level was utilitarian. A single corridor running the length of the house . . . a series of small, narrow rooms on either side.

In the house's heyday, these cell-like chambers had housed servants. She unlocked them one at a time. Several were completely empty. A few were furnished with museum pieces, as though someone had wanted to re-create their original look: small oval mirrors with mottled glass, shallow washbasins and pitchers, spindly chairs, and peeking out from beneath monastic beds, white porcelain chamber pots.

She could almost see the poor, downtrodden girls who had found a bit of rest here at the end of a long day's toil.

The last two rooms at the end of the hall, one on the left and one on the right, did not open with her third-floor key. Confused, she glanced at each lock again. The hardware on both resembled every other doorknob assembly she had tried.

She flipped through the jumble of keys on the ring and found a small brass skeleton key that was unmarked. She inserted it into the opening of the door on the left, and to her surprise it clicked and turned smoothly, allowing her to open the next-to-last door.

Perhaps she had been expecting more, but the room was much like the others. The only furnishings were a small iron bed with a sagging mattress and, at the foot of that, a large wooden chest.

The mahogany box was easily five feet long and two feet wide, and about thirty inches high. The entire lid was covered with deeply carved images of people and flowers and animals. The figures were primitive, reminiscent of African art.

And the chest was locked.

With a sigh of frustration, she set to work locating the key. She went through the entire ring twice before admitting that the appropriate key simply wasn't there. She should just forget the mysterious box and go back downstairs, where it was warm and the dust didn't make her sneeze.

But her curiosity had become an obsession. She returned to the main floor of the house and made herself eat lunch. A banana and cheese and crackers would suffice for the moment. Afterward, she selected an assortment of items from the utensil drawer and climbed the stairs once again.

As a thief, she would have been a dismal failure. Surely picking a simple lock shouldn't have been so difficult. It took twenty minutes and some mild profanity before the stubborn mechanism finally opened.

She lifted the heavy lid with trepidation, all sorts of surmises racing through her mind as to what she might uncover. At first glance, she was disappointed. She wasn't sure what she had expected . . . whips and chains? The thought made her giggle.

Nothing so titillating met her curious gaze. The contents appeared to be nothing more than stacks of black plastic DVD boxes, with no marking of any kind on the outside.

She picked one at random and opened it. To her surprise, the customary label she would have expected to see on the outside was instead attached inside the front cover of the box.

She stared at the picture, shocked. *The Countess's Revenge.* There was no doubt about the contents. The countess was dressed in what was surely not appropriate attire for a woman of her station, and the man kneeling at her feet was a gentleman in name only.

She picked up another and then another. *An Innocent Ravaged. Four Men and a Lady. Gift for a Duke. In the Hands of Savages.* Each photo and title was more outlandish than the last.

Her heart was beating fast with her guilt and excitement. Why had Trevor never mentioned these to her? Did he think she would disapprove? Or was this a private place where he came to satisfy himself when she had not been able to give him what he needed?

For an anguished moment her confidence as a female, as a lover, waned. After all, she was woefully ignorant in so many of the more sophisticated lovemaking techniques her husband had shown her. Perhaps her naïveté became too much for him after a while, and he was forced to seclude himself here in this stark little room to find release by his own hand.

She breathed deeply, her fists clenched, her lips trembling. No. Wait. She was being paranoid. There wasn't even any DVD player in this room. The disks were useless in here.

As her panic faded, her confusion increased. With rare exceptions, she couldn't think of a single time when Trevor might have had the opportunity to take one of these downstairs and watch it.

Possibly when she had taken a two-month aerobics course. Twice a week she had driven herself into town for some much-needed exercise. Perhaps while she was away, Trevor had been getting exercise of another kind, a sexual workout.

She picked up several other boxes, examining them more carefully. About half were printed in English. The others were French or Spanish or Japanese. A couple appeared to be in some kind of Scandinavian language. When she took a look at the copyright information, she realized that the DVDs were dated recently and originated in cities all over Europe.

They looked expensive and high-quality.

Leaving the room in disarray, she grabbed one of the boxes and took it to her bedroom. In the armoire, Trevor had installed a blessedly simple TV/DVD combo. She took the disk from the box, inserted it in the player, and sat on the bed with the remote in her hand.

Her cheeks were hot, and she hadn't even turned the damned thing on yet.

Fifteen minutes later, her mouth hanging open and her panties damp, she admitted to herself with some chagrin that her sophisticated, sometimes mysterious husband had some explaining to do.

No longer able to persuade herself that she was going to turn off the TV, she dropped the remote and got comfortable on the bed. The countess had stripped to a heavy gold satin merry widow and was enthusiastically whipping the man who knelt at her feet.

If the pleasurable agony on her victim's face was anything to go by, he was in heaven.

Each slice of the whip made him flinch realistically. Dani felt a combination of revulsion and arousal. The countess's full lips were cruel, her obsidian-eyed gaze narrow and implacable.

Dani was mesmerized. The setting was lush and evocative . . . a silken ottoman, heavy brocade drapes, a massive fireplace in the background.

The man began breathing heavily. His bare ass was crisscrossed with red stripes. Suddenly he stumbled to his feet and snatched the whip from his mistress's hand. He jerked her against his chest and kissed her hard, easily subduing her with his masculine strength.

She fought like a madwoman, kicking and scratching and trying to get her knee to his groin. He laughed breathlessly and carried her to the nearby settee, tossing her down and lodging himself firmly between her splayed legs.

For one heated moment their gazes clashed, hers now strangely vulnerable, his triumphant. He murmured something, but it was in French, and Dani couldn't translate. The countess spit out what was obviously a curse.

The man, goaded beyond measure, entered her swiftly. Her face reflected shock, refusal, and then a passion that was beautiful to watch. The two lovers mated savagely, the sounds of their arousal seemingly unfeigned. Dani watched, riveted, as the man pulled loose for a moment and forced the woman to lap her own juices from his enormous prick. Then, in a flash, he had tumbled her over and was taking her from behind.

Through it all Dani watched, barely breathing, with a scalding ache between her legs, and her heart in her throat. Before the credits even began to roll, she had closed her eyes and was fingering her damp sex, harder than usual, trying desperately to soothe the burning between her legs. She came with a choked cry, just as the countess shattered with a scream of ecstasy in her lover's arms.

When Dani looked again, the screen was blank.

It took her some time to recover. She lay curled up in the bed, feeling strangely unsettled. Trevor had shown her many fun and naughty things to do in the bedroom and beyond, but never had he shared anything of this nature with her.

It was as if he had a whole other side to him, one she had

never been permitted to glimpse. And the omission made her angry and frustrated.

She returned the DVD to the chest upstairs and straightened all the others as well. When she closed the lid, to her chagrin, the lock wouldn't refasten. *Well, hell's bells.* She'd done it now.

Eventually she gave up on fixing it and began the search for a key to the final locked room across the hall. Though she tried every one of the keys on the ring twice, none came close to fitting. The blank door mocked her, especially in light of what she had discovered.

After a half hour of fruitless effort, she was forced to give up. She carefully relocked the room with the carved chest and afterward rechecked all the rooms up and down the hall to make sure they were locked as well. She had no desire to be responsible for letting anyone stumble upon Trevor's secrets.

At three in the afternoon, Trevor called to say good night. She wasn't a very good actress, apparently, because he picked up on her unsettled mood immediately.

"What's wrong, Dani?" he asked sharply. "Are you okay?"

The very real concern in his voice soothed her hurt feelings a bit. "I'm fine," she said. "Just cranky, I guess. I miss you." It was everything she could do not to blurt out her shock and the million questions that were tumbling around in her head.

She could almost see his smile. "I'll be home tomorrow night. Not a second later."

Her lips twisted. "You have more faith in airlines than I do."

"They won't let me down," he said firmly. "They dare not."

The arrogant assurance in his voice amused her. In Trevor's world, he probably *could* force his will on a recalcitrant bureaucracy and make it bend to his wishes. It boggled the mind.

"Let's hope it doesn't come to that," she said with a chuckle.

He changed the subject abruptly, his voice ragged. "Are you going to tell me an interesting bedtime story, my love?"

Her indignation over what she had discovered warred with a desire to please her husband. He deserved to swing in the wind for keeping such a thing from her.

She gnawed on her bottom lip, wanting to refuse, needing him to feel the torment she felt.

But what good would it serve? He'd be home soon. They could have it out then.

She sighed. "There once was a beautiful maiden who served a cruel and unfeeling master. . . ."

Trevor listened to his wife's soft, sexy voice telling him a tale of passion and intrigue. His heart pounded and his balls tightened as he stroked his cock. When she got to the really juicy part, he grimaced and tried to hold back until the end of the story, but Dani was too good. Her husky murmurs were overstimulating to a man who had ached for the feel of her in his arms every moment they had been apart.

He spurted semen against his chest with a groan, and slumped back into the pillow.

She stopped midsentence, clearly aware that he had jumped the gun. "More?" she asked, knowing like Eve with the forbidden apple exactly what he was incapable of refusing.

"In a minute," he said quietly. "Give me sixty seconds to recover."

When they finally hung up, Trevor turned off the lamp and lay quietly in the darkness, vaguely uneasy for some reason. Dani had been loving and sensual on the phone, her erotic verbal prowess as amazing as her other gifts in that category.

But she hadn't made any effort to pleasure herself the way they had done jointly the evening before. Well, evening for her. It had definitely been morning for him. And oh, what a morning. He'd had a devil of a time concentrating on work after that.

He was in Rome now, with one more stop in London tomorrow before flying home. Business had gone smoothly, though with no credit to him. He'd been distracted and jittery. Luck more than skill had borne him through the day's negotiations.

He missed his wife. For a man who had made self-sufficiency an art, the admission was humbling. He'd been self-reliant since the age of sixteen, when his parents had initiated an extremely nasty and very public divorce. They'd had no qualms about dragging their only child into the middle of it. The family's dirty laundry had been aired in major newspapers all over Europe.

For a young teenager at a vulnerable age, the gossip and no-toriety had been incredibly painful, especially on top of the dis-solution of his family. The world as he had known it existed no more.

In the aftermath, he'd taken himself off to boarding school and left the only home he had ever known. Although it was heart-wrenching to leave, the knowledge that staying would have been equally painful made it easier.

From that moment on, he'd had very little contact with his parents. He'd done well in school, and when he went out into the world on his own, the family money had greased wheels. He was smart, driven, and successful. In very little time at all, he was able to surround himself with the privacy and anonymity he craved.

His wealth had bought him protection, but it had never been able to replace the family and the home he had once known. Only Dani had the power to do that. He'd seen it in her eyes from the beginning. The warmth. The caring. The fierce protectiveness that would keep safe what was hers. Dani was his salvation.

He rolled onto his stomach and buried his face in a pillow, wishing he had the scent of her in his head. The ache in his body transcended the physical. His soul bled for her. And after to-morrow, he was damned if he would leave her again.

Dani told herself she would not return to the room upstairs. After Trevor's call, she kept busy with one thing and another.

She spent some time outdoors puttering in the flower beds she was determined to get started. The bleak old house needed some color and beauty to soften its exterior.

Trevor had helped her plant several climbing roses, but it would be some time before they made any perceptible impact on the stone walls. In the meantime she had turned her attention to petunias, pansies, chrysanthemums, and begonias.

Because of the sheer size of the house, it was going to take lots of blooms to do the trick. She was adding to her little garden a bit at a time, and she was pleased with her progress.

She showered and changed clothes when she was finished and decided to drive herself into the nearby town for dinner. It was a small dot on the map, but the people were friendly, if a little curious. They must have seen Trevor from time to time over the years, and she wondered what they thought of him.

She wandered through the small bookstore, purchasing a cup of coffee and a baby book. The clerk smiled and exchanged idle conversation, but didn't ask any questions. Dani was glad. For now, she wanted the possibility of having a baby to remain a delicious secret between her and Trevor.

Trevor was more or less estranged from his parents. She supposed he would let them know if and when a baby was on the way. In her own case, there would be no need to tell anyone right away. Her parents had been killed in a car crash when she was twelve. No family member had stepped forward, so she and her two brothers had been split up and placed in foster care.

It wasn't a bad life. People had been kind to her. But she and her brothers had drifted apart and even now were not close.

She stopped by a small café and ordered the blue-plate special: meat loaf and mashed potatoes. The comfort food was just what she needed. She doubted whether Trevor had ever even tasted meat loaf. Perhaps she'd introduce him to the dish sometime and see if he liked it.

By seven forty-five, she could no longer think of any reason to linger. She paid the check and returned to her car for the drive home.

She'd left a number of lights on, and in the gathering gloom the house actually seemed to be welcoming her. She watched a couple of programs on BBC and then wrote a letter to her college roommate. She would save the news about hoping to get pregnant for later, but in this note she was chatty and lighthearted, describing the house and her attempts at cultivating a green thumb.

At ten o'clock she stood in the doorway to their suite and frowned. She might as well admit it. She wanted another peek at Trevor's stash.

Feeling guilty and naughty and more than a little excited, she retraced her earlier steps until she stood at the top of the stairs. The atmosphere in the dark, narrow hallway was far creepier than it had been in the morning. The small window at the far end of the corridor had at least allowed a bit of daylight.

Now the night hung heavy, and her vivid imagination heard

all sorts of creaks and groans. She went quickly to the far room, unlocked the door, and rummaged through the chest, selecting the first title that caught her eye: *In the Desert.*

Her skin was crawling with nervous prickles, so she left the disks all in disarray and bolted back downstairs to the safety of her own room and locked herself in. Then, feeling a bit foolish, she waited for her heartbeat to slow down.

She deliberately gathered a collection of toys and a glass jar of her favorite scented cream. Finally she put the disk in the player and settled back to watch. It was a fairly innocuous story line compared to some she had seen in the chest. A beautiful maiden was being held captive in the desert tent of a handsome sheikh.

No expense had been spared in designing the set. Silken draperies covered the walls, and a soft Oriental rug adorned the floor. The bed, of course, was the centerpiece of the story.

There was very little setup, and the language was not familiar to her. Perhaps the narrator's voice did a lead-in into the story, but already the hero was binding the woman's hands above her head.

The prisoner struggled convincingly, but the tiny mocking smile on her lips told another story. Her breasts were huge, almost spilling over the bodice of the little top she wore.

The sheikh was bare to the waist, his tanned, muscular back beautiful and strong. He wore traditional loose-fitting trousers, gathered at the ankle, but he stood by the bed and shed them almost immediately, revealing a fully erect cock that looked as though it meant business. His gaze was intent on his prize.

The girl shrieked, her wide eyes riveted to the rampant penis. The man seized her hips and ripped the fragile fabric that covered her legs. Then he tore away her top and left her bare and writhing on the silk-covered mattress. The forward momentum of the movie stopped for a moment as the camera zoomed in on the woman's breasts and genitals. The camera shots were subtle, revealing everything, but managing an artsy, slightly fuzzy depiction.

Even so, the woman's arousal was impossible to miss. Her dark brown nipples were tight and hard, and her kohl-lined eyes were heavy-lidded with desire. Between her widely spread legs, her soft folds glistened with moisture. It was telling that even though her legs were not bound in any way, she was open and ready for the siege that was sure to come.

Next the camera panned down the man's body, his broad shoulders, narrow waist, and impressive prick. He rubbed the head, spreading the single drop of moisture in slow strokes. Then he positioned himself between his captive's thighs and spoke soothingly to her.

The dialogue was completely unnecessary. It was plain to see her eager capitulation. She closed her eyes, her arms straining against the bindings at her wrists, her well-endowed chest heaving.

He slid two jewel-colored pillows beneath her butt. Now her

pussy was lewdly on display. He touched her with a fingertip, teasing her clitoris. Her hips lifted involuntarily.

The man pressed forward. The woman's mouth opened in a silent cry. He paused for a moment and massaged his balls. They hung huge and heavy between his legs. His face twisted in concentration. He plunged deep, almost dislodging the pillows.

The woman's head was thrown back, her body arched in supplication. He grabbed her hips and slammed into her, faster and faster. The heavy sounds of their breathing needed no translation.

They each strained for the summit, broken cries from her, harsh grunts from him. And then they climaxed almost simultaneously, shuddering and crying out and sighing in release.

Chapter Three

———❦———

Dani muted the TV for the last few seconds of the erotic scene. She couldn't stand it anymore. In real life there was nothing remotely romantic or sexy about rape. But in these brief films, it was clear that the woman was a willing participant. A proud, confident woman, perhaps, who enjoyed the forbidden thrill of letting a strong lover subdue her. And in the man's face you could see the yearning, the craving to make her his.

Watching these had been a mistake. She felt as if she were cheating on her husband. She felt terribly guilty for the hot, drugging pleasure that pumped through her veins, that centered between her legs and threatened to consume her.

With a groan she ripped off her nightgown and rolled to her back. She opened the jar of cream and swirled her finger deep in the scented lotion. Her breath caught in her throat as she smeared a dollop on each of her aching nipples. The thick substance felt cold as ice against her burning skin. She rubbed and probed and pinched, feeding the beast that rode her back.

When that wasn't enough, she took the vibrator and plunged it deeply into her throbbing sex, rotating it savagely, closing her eyes and seeing the sheikh screw his captive. Her climax came hard and fast, ripping a startled cry from her throat and rolling through her body like a freight train.

When it was over, hot tears spilled from her eyes and rolled down her cheeks to dampen her pillow.

Trevor whistled jauntily as he strode through the Salt Lake City airport. One more connecting flight to Portland, and he'd soon be with his love. He was so close to home he could taste it.

During the last leg of his journey, he relaxed in his roomy first-class seat and tried to nap. But sleep was the farthest thing from his mind. With his eyes closed he could see Dani clearly, the welcome on her animated face, her quicksilver body leaning into his as he embraced her. His cock hardened predictably, and he shifted restlessly, aching to be with his sexy wife.

On the drive home from the airport, he briefly regretted buying a house so remote and far from the city. It was now costing him precious minutes in his quest to reunite with the woman he loved.

When he finally pulled into the drive, it was just after nine o'clock. Lights blazed from every window on the first floor, beckoning him, luring him in. He grabbed his suitcase and attaché out of the backseat and ran up the front steps.

When he tripped and nearly fell on the top step, it shocked him. He stood stock-still, breathing heavily, his heart pounding. This eager-schoolboy act wasn't his normal approach, and suddenly he felt uneasy. He'd been gone only three days. Dani would think he was crazy if he busted into the house like a hormonal adolescent.

He remained there on the porch for several long, quiet minutes, collecting himself, reaching for calm. When he felt like he had a measure of control, he unlocked the front door and let himself in.

Abandoning his bags in the front hall, he sought out his wife. He found her in the kitchen. Her instant smile reassured him, but he thought she appeared tentative in her welcome. Or was he projecting his own fears onto her? He purposely hovered in the doorway. "Hello, Dani."

Her smile widened a bit, seemed a bit more genuine. "You're here. Good. Are you hungry? I baked some chicken and wild rice. I wasn't sure what time zone your stomach would be in."

The delicious aroma made his belly clench in hunger, but

other, more pressing needs prevailed. He shrugged, gripping the doorframe with white-knuckled hands. "I'll probably wake up at four a.m. starving," he said wryly. "I can always nuke it then."

She nodded. "Okay."

He watched her move around the kitchen, putting away the meal she had so thoughtfully prepared. His gaze caressed her ass as she bent to lift the casserole out of the oven. He studied her flushed cheeks, the wisps of hair escaping the careless knot on top of her head. He eyed the simple cotton knit top that outlined her sweet breasts. It was pink, like cotton candy.

His mouth was dry, his knees locked in a desperate attempt not to go to her and jump on her like a ravenous lion.

He cleared his throat. "The flower beds look nice." He'd caught them in his headlights.

She smiled more fully, her face pleased. "Thanks. I'm making progress."

She poured him a cup of decaf without asking and brought it to him. "Here you go. I've never yet had airline coffee that was any good."

This close he could see the clear gloss on her rosy lips. He could smell her familiar perfume. His hand shook, nearly spilling the hot liquid.

He took a quick swig, thankful for his asbestos tongue. "Thanks, honey," he muttered, wondering how long it would take to drag those stylish jeans to her knees. Had she noticed his hard-on?

She moved away, running a sponge over the last counter and turning out the lights. She brushed past him, intending, no doubt, to head for the den, where they often relaxed in the evenings.

He grabbed her arm, setting his cup down on the nearest surface. "Wait," he muttered. "I haven't even had a hello kiss."

He drew her into his arms slowly, stretching out the beautiful anticipation that held him in thrall. She nestled close, but still he sensed an unfamiliar tension in her. Later he would examine the cause.

Now he just wanted to fuck her.

His mouth moved over hers and he kissed her deeply, trying to curb his hunger. Her tongue played lazily with his. Her hands grasped the lapels of his jacket.

He felt himself start to lose it and drew back an inch or so, but Dani's hips moved restlessly against his, making a red haze blur his vision.

With one rapid movement he lowered her zipper and ripped her jeans to her ankles. Her shocked gasp was lost in his growl of impatience. He lifted her with one arm around her waist and put her facedown over a bar stool. Freeing his prick, he shoved into her from behind, thrusting as deeply as he could.

God, he needed this. Her hot, silky sheath milked him like a tight glove, making his head swim. His cock swelled even more. Dani's hands clasped the rungs of the stool, bracing her weight as he pumped repeatedly. Her hair loosened and fell around her face.

The curve of her butt was his anchor, his fingers digging deeply into her flesh. He felt his climax overtake him like a rushing wave, and he gave a great shout and emptied himself into her pussy until he felt like he might pass out.

When his legs began to quiver in earnest, he slipped from her body and lifted her into his arms, her pants still around her ankles. As he murmured words of apology for taking her so abruptly, he carried her to the den and slumped onto the sofa with her cuddled in his lap. He pulled an afghan over her legs reluctantly. It was a shame to cover up those beautiful limbs.

Dani had built a fire earlier, and it crackled and popped, giving out warmth and beauty, just like his wife. They sat there in silence forever, it seemed. Dani's head was tucked against his shoulder. Her legs were curled against his hip, and one of his hands played lazily with her swollen pussy.

She moved restlessly in his arms. He was pretty sure she hadn't had an orgasm. The jerk who screwed her hadn't given her a chance.

He hugged her tightly. "God, I missed you." He no longer cared about hiding the depths of what he was feeling. He was wrung out, vulnerable, quietly aching for her reassurance that she had missed him even a fraction as much.

She murmured something that wasn't quite an answer. He bent his head. "What, honey?"

She pulled back, her gray eyes dark and stormy. "I found your stash of porn," she said, resentment edging the accusation. "Why did you never tell me about it?"

Trust Dani to confront him directly. She never tiptoed around his feelings. He had wondered how long it would take her to stumble upon his collection. In fact, he'd become a bit impatient with her lack of curiosity about the third floor.

"It's about time."

He felt her go still with shock. Had she been expecting an apology? Or even worse, remorse? Not bloody likely. The only reason he hadn't introduced her to his wide-ranging assortment of films in the first place was that he thought it would be more fun for her to discover them on her own. But it hadn't occurred to him that she might do so while he was gone.

She looked up at him, her eyes cool. "You wanted me to find them?"

He shrugged. "Why else would I give you a key?"

That stopped her for a moment. She scrambled off his lap, straightening her clothes and then pacing across the room and back. "I had to break the lock on the chest." Her chin jutted, daring him to complain.

He stifled a grin. "The key to the chest was on the windowsill. I thought you would see it."

"Oh." She looked so adorably guilty, he wanted to hug her.

He stretched his arms along the back of the sofa and kicked off his shoes. It felt damned good to be home. He lifted an eyebrow. "Well, what did you think?"

She flushed as pink as her shirt. Her gaze darted away from his, and she shoved her hands in her pockets. "Um . . . well." She stopped, and he saw her swallow. Now he understood her cool tone on the phone yesterday, her almost distant greeting.

He frowned. "Are you disappointed in me? Shocked? Repulsed?" He held his breath for her answer. She was so adventurous in their bed, it had truly never occurred to him that she might disapprove.

She shook her head violently. "Of course not."

"But . . ."

She sighed, finally looking at him. Beneath her thin shirt and thinner bra he saw her pert nipples.

He probed again, impatient to hear what she had to say. "But . . ."

She blinked, clearly flustered. "I was surprised."

"That's all?"

"And intrigued."

That sounded more promising. "Did you watch one?"

"No."

It took him aback. He'd been sure she would.

"I watched two." Her eyes were bright . . . and still that note of challenge was in her voice, as though somehow she expected censure from him.

His lips lifted in a smile. "Which ones?"

She lifted her chin. "I'd rather not say. It's embarrassing."

He cocked his head. "Why?"

She looked frustrated now. "Do we have to talk about this?"

That wiped the smile from his face. "Not if you don't want to," he said quietly, disappointment flooding his stomach. He stood up and fastened his pants. "I think I could use some dinner now."

"Wait."

He turned around, trying to mask his chagrin. Dani's eyes were filled with turbulent emotion. "We have some unfinished business," she said quietly. "Or are you planning to be a selfish lover from now on?"

He flushed. In his eagerness to know if she'd enjoyed the provocative videos, he'd momentarily overlooked the fact that his lovely wife hadn't been satisfied. "My apologies," he said, making a half bow. "Consider me at your service."

She pulled her hands from her pockets and pointed an imperious finger. "Kneel in front of the sofa."

He lifted an intrigued eyebrow. Dani seldom took the lead in their lovemaking, at least, not at first. When they were deeply engrossed in each other's bodies, she was more eager, less reserved. But now she clearly intended to be in the driver's seat.

After a brief moment of hesitation, he did as she commanded and knelt in front of the long mocha leather divan.

Dani watched him carefully, her usual easy-to-read expression guarded. While he watched, she shed her clothes without ceremony.

He didn't need a provocative striptease. Her matter-of-fact

movements stirred him more than the most erotic dance performance. When she was nude, his chest rose and fell in a sigh. Now that he had slaked the knife edge of his frustrated arousal, he was better able to appreciate what he'd neglected earlier.

She was as graceful as a ballerina. Her narrow waist flared into barely curved hips and long, slender thighs. Her shining midnight black hair fell across her toned shoulders and small breasts.

He licked his lips as she approached him. His heartbeat picked up speed, and already his cock flexed and swelled.

She scooted around him and settled herself on the soft, plump cushions, propping her feet on the coffee table at his back and bracketing him with her legs.

She leaned back and closed her eyes. "You may proceed."

Her haughty little comment surprised a sharp bark of laughter from him. She seemed completely comfortable, and while he liked her sensual confidence, *he* wasn't comfortable at all. He was getting hot and bothered all over again.

He leaned forward and licked the inside of her left knee, barely touching the skin. She shivered, although the fire made the room plenty warm. He repeated the caress inside her other knee. Almost imperceptibly her stance widened another inch.

Ever so slowly he worked his way up her inner thighs, wetting two or three inches at a time with his tongue, first one side, then the other. The closer he came to the juncture of her legs, the more she tensed.

He never varied the press of his tongue. He kept the lazy strokes light and even. Now that he was no longer crazed by the hunger of abstinence, he realized she had bathed for him, perhaps right before he arrived. The lush scent of magnolia blossoms clung to her skin.

His need to take her again built quickly, urging him to hurry, but he forced himself to maintain the languid pace. Dani was breathing heavily now, her eyes closed, her lips parted. A delicate flush stained her throat and chest. Her hands pressed, palms down, into the cushions. Her back arched, her hips lifting into his touch.

When he was so close to the lush folds of her sex that she had to feel his warm breath on her clit, he backed away and began using his hands to massage her feet and calves. Her eyes flew open as she inhaled sharply in shocked astonishment.

She glared at him. "You stopped?"

He continued his deep strokes, feeling her leg muscles soften and relax beneath his fingers. "I didn't stop," he said with an innocent frown. "I merely changed positions. The feet are a very erogenous zone. I thought you knew that."

Her eyes narrowed. "Your timing sucks." He hit a tender spot and she gasped.

He smiled slyly. "See. I was right."

Her hands were clenched in fists now, drumming restlessly against the poor abused cushions. "I would greatly appreciate it if you moved your attentions north," she said in a prissy, polite voice.

"If you insist." He raised up off his heels and leaned forward, treating her collarbones to the same slow tongue assault he'd been using moments earlier. In this position, his erection bumped against her leg.

He bit gently at her neck, leaving a mark.

Dani whimpered. "South." It was barely a whisper.

He licked her nipples, then sucked them one at a time deep into his mouth, tugging until she groaned and trembled.

"Farther south," she mumbled.

He slid his tongue down her rib cage to her belly and played with her navel. She had the cutest little belly button, and he nibbled at it with teasing little nips. Dani moaned, her hands coming up to grab handfuls of his hair. "South." She was hoarse now, her breath coming in short pants.

He nuzzled the pretty fuzz of hair at the top of her mound. He licked his way down the crease where her leg met her torso. And then the other side.

"Bastard," she croaked, trembling uncontrollably.

He laughed softly. He blew on her clit, then licked the moist skin on either side. He could feel the tension coiled so tightly inside her.

And then he ran his tongue over her clit. One light pass and then two firm strokes, and she came apart in his embrace, feverishly pressing her aching flesh against his face until the last shuddering peak dropped her back to earth.

He sat back and wiped his mouth on his sleeve. "The hors d'oeuvres were delicious, my pet."

With horny dexterity, he unzipped his trousers for the second time, reversed their positions, and thrust upward into her swollen pussy. He altered the angle a bit, reaching for that special spot high and inside her cunt. She flinched and groaned, bearing down on his cock. He held her hips, rocking forward again.

Dani's hair tumbled around her face. Her hands rested on his shoulders. "I should send you out of town more often," she mumbled.

"Hell, no," he muttered. "I barely survived this time." He eased out and back in, trying to pace himself—no easy trick, with every cell in his body bearing down on the finish line.

She pressed her forehead against his. "Don't be such a baby. It was only three days."

"Three days, three hours. Doesn't matter. I can't seem to kick this addiction."

"To sex?"

He dropped his head back, his chest heaving. "To you," he admitted roughly, his eyes closed. And then he showed her just how little he cared about rehabilitation when the rewards of giving in to temptation were so damned good.

Dani lay beside her husband in their big bed and listened to the sounds of his breathing. He'd surprised her tonight. For a brief moment the suave, sophisticated man she'd fallen in love with had revealed a vulnerability that touched her deeply.

He'd missed her. Badly.

She wasn't sure why that seemed so significant. Perhaps even now she wasn't entirely secure in his love. He'd experienced so much of life, of carnal pleasure, it was sometimes difficult to believe that he wanted and needed her as much as she did him.

He slept like the dead, poor baby. He was exhausted, and no wonder. He'd traversed too many time zones in too short a time span to be adjusted anywhere.

She, on the other hand, slept fitfully. She kept waking and reaching out to make sure he was beside her. Finally, at three a.m. she gave up trying to sleep and stared up at the ceiling, thinking about their earlier awkward conversation.

It still bothered her somehow that Trevor claimed he meant for her to find the DVDs. Why not just show them to her in the first place? Unless he was afraid, somehow. Come to think of it, he *had* seemed wary when she confronted him about them. Perhaps letting her stumble upon them on her own was his way of testing the waters.

He had definitely seemed subdued when she refused to tell him about the ones she had watched. She wasn't sure why she refused. She had never been shy around her husband, at least, not since the very early days of their lovemaking.

But her own reaction to the films made her uneasy and almost ashamed. Weren't porn movies something that men enjoyed?

Women weren't supposed to be visually stimulated in that way, right? Women were expected to turn up their noses and talk about exploitation and stuff like that. What did it say about her if she became so aroused by watching something so politically incorrect?

By the time each movie ended, she had been so hungry for sexual release, she was shaking and practically incoherent. She couldn't admit that to her husband . . . could she?

She stroked a hand down his back, remembering the steely-eyed countess. For a brief moment tonight, when Trevor had so willingly knelt at her feet, she had contemplated what it would feel like to have him at her mercy. That one fleeting thought had been almost enough to trigger her orgasm, especially since she had been so turned on by how her husband greeted her in the kitchen.

Seeing him that hungry had reminded her of the man in the movie. Did she have it in her to ever mete out punishment? Even thinking about it in the abstract made her lower abdomen fill with heat. And what about the other story? The sheikh and his captive. That might be even more fun to act out.

Not to mention the hundred or so other titillating tales resting so innocently in the erotic Pandora's box at the top of the stairs.

And then she thought once again about Trevor's claim that he had given her the key to the room on purpose. That he wanted her to find his collection.

But what about the last room? She had tried every key on the ring . . . twice. And none of them fit that final door. Why would he have so subtly led her upstairs and revealed his secrets and omitted one mysterious room?

Perhaps because it was nothing more than a storage area for broken knickknacks and hard-to-part-with mementos. On the other hand, Trevor had never struck her as being a pack rat. He was almost obsessively neat. His life and his living space were ordered. Controlled. She wondered at times if her occasional messiness bothered him. If so, he had never mentioned it.

So if the room wasn't full of clutter, what else could it be?

The more she thought about it, the more she wanted to wake her sleeping husband and demand answers. But why should he cooperate, when she had been so closemouthed about watching the videos?

Her hands went to her breasts, stroking them absently. She closed her eyes and she could still feel the tug of his mouth on her sensitive flesh, still experience the jagged arc of desire that connected her nipples to her womb.

She rolled to her side, wanting to wake him. He was exhausted. It wouldn't be fair.

But those damned movies started playing in her head. Would she ever be able to block them? The crack of the whip . . . the man's temporary submission . . . the passionate sheikh . . . the soft, anguished cries of the helpless, bound girl.

Oh, God. It was happening again. The desperate, irrational hunger. She tried to think of something else, anything else. Her flower beds. The new nursery. Thinking about her earlier pregnancy only made it worse. Imagining Trevor's determined efforts to plant his seed deep in her womb made her tremble in remembrance.

She reached for her husband. He was sprawled on his back. Carefully she slid beneath the covers and found his soft penis. She took it in her mouth, gently licking at first, and then as he responded, sucking him deep into her throat.

He groaned. His hips lifted. He murmured in his sleep and then jerked awake. "Dani . . . ?"

She had him fully erect now, so thick and long she was unable to swallow his length. She reached between his legs and cupped his balls, scraping lightly with her fingernails. She didn't bother to speak. Her form of communication was working just fine.

With a growl that encompassed surprise and hunger and his intent to pounce, he pushed her to her back and rolled on top of her, sinking his cock deep.

She cried out, feeling torn apart by violent pleasure. She was close to climax already, and she urged him into a quicker rhythm. "Faster," she panted. "Harder."

"Anything for a lady," he grunted, his arms corded with muscles as he braced his weight above her.

He thrust rapidly, sending them both hurtling toward a release that should have been gentle and sweet. They'd each come twice before.

But nothing about this mating was soft or sentimental. It was raw and urgent and intense. She wrapped her legs around his back, tilting her hips to drive him deeper. He hissed a curse and shoved all the way in, hovering there as he reached between them and teased her clit.

She cried out and went rigid, her climax blinding her to his shouted release as he collapsed in her arms.

In the fleeting moments before she tumbled into sleep, she kissed his chin and rubbed her cheek against his. "Welcome home, Trevor."

Chapter Four

She roused to the unmistakable aroma of coffee from fresh-ground beans. Trevor held a china cup carefully, wafting it under her nose. "Time to get up, sleepyhead. The day's a-wastin'."

She yawned and stretched, ruefully aware that the bright sunlight pouring though the window meant it was midmorning.

Trevor set the cup on the bedside table and smoothed the hair back from her cheeks. The look on his face made her heart clench. Such open tenderness from a man renowned for his cold, unemotional business persona made her both grateful and humble.

She lifted a hand and twined her fingers with his. "I liked the movies," she said quietly. "The ones upstairs. I was thinking about them last night when I . . ." She stopped and bit her lip, still not quite able to be blasé about her reactions.

He grinned. "You mean when you woke me up and had your wicked way with me?"

She tucked her chin. "Yeah."

He leaned over and kissed her on the lips. "I'm glad." Then he glanced at his watch. "I'd love to climb back in bed with you, sweetheart, but I've got a conference call in ten minutes. I left you some toast and bacon warming in the oven."

And then he was gone.

Well, pooh. She'd screwed up her courage and admitted that she enjoyed watching his naughty European sex flicks, and he had barely even noticed. *Okay, fine.* That was that. The room upstairs could stay locked indefinitely as far as she was concerned.

She showered and dressed in a simple skirt and blouse and low-heeled sandals. She had a doctor's appointment, and since she'd slept half the day away, she was in danger of being late. When she poked her head into Trevor's large, high-tech study, he jumped to his feet, determined to go with her.

She pushed him back in his chair. "Stay here. Get some work done. All they're going to do at this visit is a general exam. Nothing exciting, I promise."

He glanced back at the computer screen, clearly distracted. "If you're sure."

She kissed the top of his head, ruffling his hair. "I'm sure."

As she drove into town, she wondered if she should push the issue of Trevor's hidden collection any further. Last night he seemed interested in her reactions, but this morning when she confessed what she really thought, he'd barely acknowledged it. She was still learning about her complicated husband. It would take time.

Her ob-gyn was a white-haired gentleman who reminded her of Santa Claus. He was a renowned gardener, so they discussed his tomato plants while he examined her. When the exam was over and the nurse stepped out of the room for a moment, Dani asked the question that had been tormenting her for several weeks.

"Dr. Nelson, I've been wondering.... When I finally do get pregnant again, will it still be okay to...I mean...um... should I abstain...?"

His smile was professional but kind. "Are you asking about sex, Mrs. Shapelli?"

She felt her cheeks heat. "Yes."

He folded her chart and tucked it away. "You didn't miscarry because you had sex. Sex won't hurt the fetus. And in fact, it's perfectly natural for a woman your age and in your excellent fitness to experience an increased interest in intimacy during pregnancy. In fact, many patients find their sex lives particularly enjoyable well into their eighth month, if there are no complicating factors."

"And it's safe?" Some of her anxiety must have shone through in her voice.

He handed her a lollipop with a mischievous grin. "Nothing

that doesn't hurt you will hurt the baby. Go enjoy life, Mrs. Shapelli. And enjoy food, as well. None of that silly dieting. You young women go too far sometimes."

She hopped off the table, tucking the childish treat in her skirt pocket with an answering smile. "So everything checks out? My body's okay?"

"You're a healthy, normal woman. When you and your husband are ready to try again, there is no reason to believe you shouldn't be successful."

Her clinic visit soothed the last of her fears, and she felt lighthearted and suddenly very much in need of her husband's attentions—so much so that she stopped on the way home for a bottle of wine. She wouldn't mind getting her lover a bit tipsy.

He was standing in the driveway poking at her flower beds when she drove up. He put his hands on his hips and shielded his eyes from the sun with one hand. "What took you so long? Is everything okay?"

She wrapped her arms around his neck and kissed him, leaning into his embrace and savoring the feel of his heartbeat against her breast. He was so warm. So strong. So dear. "I'm fine. I stopped for a few groceries, that's all."

He carried both of her bags, shooing her into the house in front of him. Over a late lunch they talked about this and that. Trevor told her a few more anecdotes about his trip. It was comfortable. Nice.

But Dani had her mind on the evening. She shot him a look

over her shoulder as she put the wine in to chill. "What if we grill steaks tonight? I feel like celebrating."

He smacked her on the bottom with the dish towel. "Oh? Have we won the lottery?"

She slid her arms around his waist. "I have," she murmured, meaning every word of it. She was suddenly close to tears.

"Dani?" He lifted her chin. "What is it, sweetheart?"

She sniffed, feeling weepy and horny and unbelievably happy. "I love you."

"And that makes you cry?"

"Sometimes."

He laughed and cuddled her close. "Then cry all you want, my angel, because I intend to make you as happy as I can for the rest of our lives."

The day passed by in a contented blur of mundane tasks. That evening Dani fixed baked potatoes and spinach salad to go with the steaks Trevor grilled to perfection. She'd picked up a loaf of French bread at the store, and for dessert they had fresh strawberries and sherbet. She ate sparingly, too wound up to fully appreciate the excellent meal.

They dined by candlelight. Trevor's sharp features looked almost solemn. She reached across the table for his hand. "Will you answer a personal question for me?"

He grimaced. "You don't need to hear about my first time, do you? Frankly it was embarrassing."

She laughed softly. "We can skip that. I'm not sure I even want to know."

He squeezed her fingers, his expression wry with self-deprecation. "Trust me, you don't." He took a sip of his wine. "Then what?"

She topped off his glass. "Why didn't you give me the key to the last room?"

He choked and set down the fragile glass with an appalling lack of concern for the delicate crystal. He wiped his mouth with a crisp linen napkin, clearly stalling for time.

She waited him out, trying to gauge his reaction to her blunt question, her eyes on his face.

He stood up and looked out the window. The full moon silvered the landscape with ghostly charm. He sighed. "I wanted to show it to you myself."

She frowned. "I don't understand."

He turned to face her. "When we got married, you moved into my house, with all my things."

"I told you I didn't mind that. Most of my stuff was early garage sale."

"Maybe so, but after we got engaged, I decided I wanted us to find one place in this big old house that was *ours*. Together. So I began making plans, ordering things, making a spot for us."

"But, Trevor, you've never even taken me to the third floor."

He shrugged. "I wasn't sure I was ready . . . that we were ready."

The fog cleared. Whatever was in that room was something

very special. "You weren't sure about me," she said quietly. "The box of videos was some sort of a test, wasn't it?"

He grimaced. "I didn't want to push you into something that made you uncomfortable."

"And now?"

His eyes met hers, and the heat in his steady gaze would have made her knees buckle if she had been standing. He cleared his throat. "Now I want to take you there. If you're willing to go."

A sharp shiver trembled down her spine, and her mouth went dry.

"Yes," she said simply. "Please." She wasn't able to articulate more than that.

He stared at her for long moments. The house was still and quiet except for the ticking of the mantel clock. Dani could actually feel her own blood pumping through her veins.

Her stomach rolled and pitched, but in a good way. It was that feeling you get when you know beyond the shadow of a doubt that something wonderful is about to happen. When delicious possibilities fill your veins with fizzy excitement.

Trevor seemed frozen, his expression impossible to read. Had he changed his mind?

She pushed her chair back and stood up. He didn't move. She crossed to where he stood. The beautiful scene outside the window didn't merit a glance. She had eyes only for her husband.

She laid her palm against his cheek. "What's wrong, Trevor?"

Still he didn't move. His hands were in his pockets. A muscle worked in his throat. He looked down at his feet, causing her hand to fall away. "The way I feel about you scares me," he said in a raw voice.

"I don't understand."

He half turned away, and moonlight fell on his face, revealing the torment in his eyes. "I practically attacked you when I came home last night. I'm so sorry. I could have hurt you."

"But you didn't. I'm fine, Trevor. We made love. That's all."

"Over a damned bar stool," he groaned.

Remembering that particular moment brought heat to her cheeks and elsewhere. His raw, urgent hunger had aroused her to the same level of mindless need. "So what? I liked it."

"I didn't give you a chance not to." The self-loathing in his tone was a bit much.

She pinched his arm. "If I had said no, would you have stopped?"

Shock flashed across his face. "Of course."

She shrugged. "Then what's the big deal?"

He swallowed hard. "I'm afraid that if I get too aroused, I may lose control."

Suddenly she understood a bit of his dilemma. Trevor Shapelli was a man defined by control. For him to imagine otherwise would be daunting. And his fierce sexuality was almost a living, breathing entity.

She sighed. "Isn't that a big part of the pleasure and the excitement? Feeling yourself pushed beyond that limit?" Skating around the subject of what might happen when they went upstairs made her palms damp. Did she have the courage to match his eroticism?

"It's like a drug," he admitted quietly. "Almost like flying, but without being sure there's a net below to catch you."

"We'll be there for each other, Trevor. And no matter what your fears are, you would never hurt me, intentionally or otherwise. You couldn't."

He gripped her shoulders suddenly, his expression fierce. "You'll tell me? If you don't like something? If I push too hard?"

Her legs trembled. She could feel the carnal tension in his body. "I swear," she whispered.

He took her mouth then in a punishing kiss. His desperation fed her own hunger, and she went up on tiptoe to drag his face closer.

All of her emotions coalesced into one panting, feverish knot of need. She was apprehensive, but eager. Timid, but insatiably curious. Whatever surprises Trevor had for her in that locked room would only make her love him more. He had waited for her to be ready, and she was. God help her, she was.

They held hands as they went upstairs. She clung to his fingers as if it were a lifeline. The steep steps seemed twice as long, the shadows twice as deep. They stopped in front of the only door she had not been able to open, and Trevor reached in his pocket for a small metal ring from which dangled a single key.

He unlocked the door without ceremony and flipped on the lights. Her heart was beating so rapidly she was breathless. He stepped back and allowed her to enter before him. She wasn't sure what she had expected, but it wasn't this. In her crazy imagination, she had wondered if it would be some kind of weird torture chamber with iron cages and medieval implements.

The reality was so far removed from her bizarre speculations that it took her a moment to adjust. The room was lovely. Beneath her feet, plush wall-to-wall carpeting in a rich, lush crimson cushioned every step. The ceiling had been painted midnight blue, and tiny rhinestone stars glittered in the illumination of carefully concealed track lighting.

The walls were a creamy ivory. Anything darker would have made the modest room seem too small. The one window was curtainless. She peeked out and could barely see the ocean far below. Moonlight would spill in later, but for now, the pale orb rose high in the sky.

Trevor stood silently in the doorway, content to let her explore at her own pace. But his dark eyes were watchful.

She touched a thick navy velvet curtain on the far wall.

He nodded toward the ornate gold-tasseled cord. "Open it."

She pulled on the heavy braided length. The fabric gathered smoothly to the right, revealing an enormous flat television screen. Anything pictured there would seem almost life-size.

She looked at her unusually quiet companion. "For the DVDs?"

Now a small, smug grin tilted his lips. "Yes. It's the biggest one they make."

She chuckled. Boys and their toys. She tried not to think about the sheikh taking his captive on that enormous plasma expanse. It boggled the mind.

The furniture was minimal, and that was good, because anything more would have cramped the space. Beneath the window stood a small dorm-style refrigerator. In the center of the floor facing the screen was a beautiful, oversize armchair/chaise longue. She'd seen them in furniture stores. The back and arms looked like a traditional chair, but the cushion and seat extended forward so that the occupant could stretch his or her legs full-length.

The piece of furniture had obviously been specially ordered, because it was far bigger than any one of its kind she had ever seen. It was upholstered in soft velvet as well, but the expensive fabric was crimson, to match the carpet.

The only item as yet unexplored was a large armoire on the wall to the right. It appeared to be an antique. When she drew back the double doors, she saw a long column of drawers to the left and numerous articles of clothing hanging to the right.

She opened a drawer at random and looked at the assortment of items inside. She felt her face flush and she closed it rapidly.

Behind her Trevor chuckled wickedly. "Too much, too soon?" he asked gently.

She faced him, her nose wrinkled. "We'll work up to that drawer." She held out a hand. "This is incredible."

He smiled. "I'm glad you like it." He motioned toward the armoire. "Why don't you pick out something to wear, and I'll select a few movies?"

Before she could respond, he disappeared across the hall. She turned back to the chest and sorted through the garments hanging there. Merry widows. Eighteenth-century ball gowns. Baby-doll pajamas. Smoking jackets. Male and female attire of every kind.

She found an ivory satin kimono-style robe embroidered with a bloodred dragon. Trevor had obviously thought out every detail. This particular item of clothing would look beautiful against the ruby fabric of the seat. The visual stimulation was inescapable.

She slipped out of her clothes and hung them neatly. The robe was scented with some spicelike fragrance, and when she slid it over her bare skin, the brush of it was almost sexual.

When Trevor returned, his eyes skated over her body in appreciation. "Lovely," he said softly.

He shed his own clothes and picked a black silk robe that complemented her attire. Suddenly he seemed less familiar. His tanned legs below the hem of the robe were lightly covered in dark hair, and the eroticism of his bare feet sinking into the deep pile of the carpet made her weak.

He caught her staring. "What?"

Her lips trembled. "You're a beautiful man," she whispered.

His eyes flashed fire for a split second before he smiled. "I'm flattered."

Everything about his demeanor indicated casual, comfortable enjoyment of what was to come, but when she looked closely, she could see that the nonchalance was an act. Her husband was in the throes of a powerful arousal. Not that he could easily hide it when he donned the robe. His veined, brownish-red cock reared thick and strong against his belly.

She hovered uncertainly, watching as he went to the DVD system built into the wall and inserted a selection. The lights were on a dimmer switch, so he lowered them and held out a hand. "Ready?"

She bit her bottom lip, her heart in her throat. "I suppose."

He pulled her into his arms. "Such enthusiasm," he teased softly.

She burrowed into his bare chest, inhaling his familiar scent. "You must think I'm silly."

He stroked her hair. "I think you're a miracle." His hands slid beneath her robe and settled on her hips. "I think you're beautiful and kind and adventurous and sexy. But never silly."

His erection pressed into her belly. She sucked in a breath, moving as close as she was able. Could she seduce him right now? She didn't want to wait. She needed to feel him deep inside her, binding them together. No matter how many times they made love, she wanted more.

She reached for his cock.

He jerked back and grabbed her hand. "No."

She pouted. "I want you."

The cords in his neck were standing out, and streaks of red colored his cheekbones. His lips thinned in a grimace. "And you'll have me. But not yet. Give me a chance to show you how good we can be."

"What if I'm completely satisfied with the way things are now?"

He took another step back, breathing heavily. "Don't ever be satisfied, angel. It can always be better. I want you to feel pleasure so deep, it's almost pain. I want to watch your pretty eyes go wide when you slide over the edge of a cliff you never knew you could scale. I want to hear you beg for relief when the ache grips you and drags you to the edge of sanity."

Her eyes were locked on his face, her arms wrapped around her waist. His words threatened to make her fall apart. "And you can do that?"

He shrugged one shoulder, an elegant, careless motion that indicated confidence, determination. "With your permission . . . your cooperation."

She tucked her hair behind her ears, trying to look as confident as he was. "Then show me."

The look of pride on his face warmed her from the inside out. His teeth flashed white in a male grin of satisfaction. "Thank you, sweetheart."

Trevor was having a difficult time regulating his breathing. He wanted to jump her and screw her to the wall. Already his savage impulses struggled to break free. But he was determined to see this through.

He went to the fridge and took out a bottle of water. He opened the cap and drained half the contents. He focused on the mundane act, trying to rein himself in, trying not to get ahead of the game.

He managed a look at Dani. "Are you thirsty, sweetheart?"

She nodded slowly. He took the bottle to her and held it as she opened her lips and closed her eyes. "Drink," he said huskily.

She swallowed, and he wiped a drop of moisture from her chin. She opened her eyes, looking wary and uncertain. He saw her lips tremble, and against the pretty robe her nipples peaked.

He took her hand and led her to the chair. He reclined against the deep cushions, settling her with her back to his chest. He liked seeing his own legs bracketing her slender, pale limbs. His aching cock pressed against her lower back.

He untied the sash of her robe and lifted it out to the sides.

She half turned her head. "What are you doing, Trevor?"

Just inside each arm of the chair was a small brass ring barely an inch in diameter. They were covered in matching cloth, so he was pretty sure she hadn't noticed them.

He wrapped one end of the sash around her left wrist several times and secured it through the ring. He saw her fists curl, but she didn't struggle, even as he repeated the action with her opposite arm.

He leaned his cheek close to hers, his breath brushing her ear.

"During the movie you aren't allowed to touch yourself. Only I can do that."

She fidgeted briefly. "Why would I touch myself when I have you?" she asked, genuinely curious.

Her artless question made him smile quietly. "You'll see."

He kissed her cheek, drawing her more firmly into his embrace. "Comfortable?"

She sighed deeply, bending her knees and curling her legs into a relaxed position. "Of course."

He picked up the remote from where it lay wedged between the cushion and the chair.

"Then let's begin."

Chapter Five

D ani relaxed against Trevor's broad chest as the movie credits began to roll. The writing was in a foreign language, but just below what was clearly the title was an English translation: *The More the Merrier.*

Her lips twitched. *This should be fun.*

Trevor murmured in her ear, "It has subtitles I can switch on, but I think it's distracting. I'm pretty sure you can follow the plot."

She giggled, tugging lightly at her wrists. "I'll bet."

The movie opened with a city street scene. Trevor offered whispered commentary. "It's set in Amsterdam in the red-light district."

Then he fell silent as the movie unfolded. An attractive blonde meandered with an easy stride down the sidewalk. She passed cinemas that were definitely not showing Disney films, and crowded, smoky bars open to the street where men leered and whistled at her. Occasionally she paused and looked at a scrap of paper in her pocket. The background music was unfamiliar, but it seemed to suit the mood.

Finally the young woman stopped in front of what appeared to be an apartment building. Its gray plaster facade was rather ugly, and the flight of three crooked steps led up to a nondescript door.

She pressed a buzzer, and the door opened.

Dani lost sight of the action on the screen for a moment when she felt Trevor's lips nuzzle the sensitive skin just below her ear.

When he kissed the curve of her neck, she squirmed. Moisture already gathered in the folds of her sex, and Trevor had tucked her robe up around her waist so her bare bottom and legs rubbed the velvet.

She tried to concentrate. The heroine stood at a small desk in the foyer speaking quietly to an older woman who consulted a ledger. The young woman handed over a wad of money. Then her hostess led her down a dark hallway to an unmarked door.

Dani turned her head, trying to see Trevor's face. "What's happening?"

"The girl has paid for a requested sexual scenario. The room she's about to enter is called something I can't pronounce, but the rough translation is 'dream chamber.' It's a place men or women can go for entertainment."

The camera zoomed in on the girl's hand twisting the doorknob. In spite of herself, Dani's breathing quickened.

The room was vacant except for a low-to-the-floor bed. It was covered in a coarse sheet and nothing else, no blanket, no pillows.

A door at the back of the room opened, and six men entered silently. They were of similar height and were fairly ordinary-looking, three fair and three dark headed. They were completely nude, and their penises were not erect.

The girl seemed startled at first, but then she murmured a greeting. The men ignored her. They stalked forward as one, causing her to back up against the door in fright. The camera shot a close-up again, this time showing the girl's trembling lips and then her hard nipples poking through her thin blouse.

The men converged on her like a storm of testosterone, ripping and pawing at her clothes until she was nude between them.

One of the men kissed her, shoving his way closer and tipping her head back in big hands. She made little noises in her throat, but her hands came up to circle his neck. She jerked and flinched when one man fell to the floor and began to tongue her pussy.

Dani was shivering now, her knees drawn to her chest as she watched, spellbound. Trevor's hands cupped her breasts. He rolled her nipples and pinched them. A third man on the screen did the same thing to the nude girl.

Dani moved restlessly. She was burning up suddenly. The robe was so hot. But with her hands bound she couldn't take it completely off. She felt Trevor's big cock at her back, and she lifted up, intending to lean forward until he could slip inside her aching sex.

But he grasped her hips and held her down, his teeth sinking into the tender spot where her neck met her shoulder. "No, Dani," he muttered hoarsely.

Suddenly, she understood why her hands were bound. She wanted to stroke her clitoris, hard. God, she needed to come.

A cry from the screen jerked her attention back to the movie. The men were carrying her now, all six of them. They dropped her to the bed and subdued her easily when she tried to escape.

Two men seized her ankles and spread them apart at a lewd angle, revealing the woman's light thatch of hair and the slippery skin below. Two others positioned themselves at her shoulders and stretched her arms painfully wide. The fifth man rubbed his prick over her face and then shoved it between her lips.

The final man positioned himself between the girl's legs and began to move.

Dani struggled wildly. "Please, Trevor, let me go. I want to touch you. I want you to touch me. Oh, God." She was frantic.

The ache between her legs was overwhelming. She wanted to climb the walls. She couldn't stand this torture.

Trevor's hand smoothed her damp brow. "I know I'm not hurting you, Dani. Try to relax. Enjoy the end of the picture."

She tugged uselessly at her bound arms, desperate to free herself. Just one touch. That was all. One quick stroke where she needed it most and she could fly.

Trevor held her face between his hands, forcing her to look at the screen. "Watch them," he commanded softly.

The implacable tone of his voice let her know he was serious. Shaking, trembling, desperate for release, she slumped against him and watched in shocked amazement as the drama unfolded.

The sixth man was large. The camera zoomed again, recording the woman's drenched labia clinging to the thick erection that parted her with inexorable force. The man in her mouth abandoned his position and moved around the bed until he could suck on her breasts one at a time.

Now the camera was on the girl's face. Subtitles would have been superfluous at this point. Anyone who had ever experienced the aching quest for completion would understand. The woman's eyes were open wide, her face flushed with color.

Though she had to know it was a vain effort, she continued to struggle against the men who held her down. The man fucking her groaned and shifted into high gear, making the bed shake with his mighty thrusts.

The woman screamed. Her back arched. And she climaxed with a beautiful, shuddering moan of ecstasy that trailed off into almost silent whimpers.

The male and female locked in the carnal embrace lay still. The other five exited quietly. Moments later the last man recovered himself enough to roll off the bed, and then he, too, was gone.

In the final frame, the camera zoomed in one last time and captured the woman's smile of contentment.

And then the screen went dark.

Trevor cupped her breasts. "Tell me what you feel," he said, his lips at her ear.

She rarely cursed, but the need to do so now almost overrode years of polite behavior. "Let me go."

He thumbed her nipples. "Tell me, little love, tell me."

She sucked in a hiccuped breath and tried to concentrate on his voice. "I feel like I'm being torn apart."

"How?"

She couldn't see his face, and the room now was almost completely dark. His voice was the only thing she could cling to. "Like everything inside me is struggling to get out. Like my veins and bones are melting."

"And between your legs?"

She sobbed. "I can't bear it," she moaned. "Please let me come."

He trailed a necklace of kisses from one side of her nape to the other. "Tell me about the movie. Did you like it?"

"Did you?" she whispered, stalling for time.

She felt him shrug. "It's not one of my favorites. But I thought you might find it . . . interesting."

She bit her lip.

He nudged her. "Dani? The movie?"

His voice was as calm and serene as the surface of a lake on a windless day. Did he expect her to critique it like the latest Bond picture? She cleared her throat. "It was . . ."

He pinched her nipples, making her cry out, more in surprise than anything else. He nibbled her earlobe. "It was arousing . . . Is that what you're trying to say?"

She nodded jerkily. She could almost climax with his fingers on her breasts.

He massaged her belly, playing with the curls at the very top of her mound. "The woman wanted to be subdued. You saw that, right?"

"Yes." She lifted her hips, trying to force him lower.

"Do you think you might ever enjoy being held down? Restrained?"

Her fingernails cut into her palms, and her wrists ached. "Possibly." The whispered admission was little more than a thread of sound.

Trevor traced her collarbones. "Not by the six men, of

course," he said in a conversational tone. "I'm not that generous. But I might enjoy having my lovely wife at my mercy."

The heat between her legs became a stab of flame. Her lips trembled. "Trevor." She couldn't even articulate her plea.

Behind her she felt him move, and suddenly he was climbing over the arm of the chair, leaving her abandoned and awkwardly bound. With him gone, she couldn't quite lean back in comfort.

He saw her predicament and retrieved a pillow from the floor of the armoire. As he tucked it behind her back, he kissed her cheek.

Dani lay helpless, listening to the muffled noises he made as he searched for something. At the back of the room near the door, one dim light still burned. It was enough to enable Trevor to see what he was doing, but not enough for her to be able to see him very well.

She closed her eyes and tried to breathe deeply. Every muscle in her body was tensed. She concentrated on relaxation techniques, letting one part of her body at a time go slack. She was congratulating herself on her success when Trevor returned to the chair.

He touched her hair. "Keep your eyes closed."

She nodded, but his quiet command sparked a new flame. She felt his hands at her thighs, spreading them. She flashed to the woman in the movie, watching her being violated.

Suddenly, she gasped as a thick object pressed at her entrance. She jerked. "Trevor . . ."

He brushed her eyelids. "No peeking," he said huskily. "Just feel."

Unfortunately, she wasn't a very obedient wife, it seemed. Involuntarily, her eyes opened long enough to see an almost grotesquely large, leather-covered penis in her husband's hands. Her legs tensed. Clearly it wouldn't fit.

Trevor sighed as though disappointed in her. He picked up a blindfold from the floor and secured it over her eyes. Then he caught the back of her head in one large palm and pulled her close for a hungry kiss. Despite his outward demeanor, the kiss was desperate.

Again he whispered in her ear, "Relax. Let yourself feel."

The first was impossible. The second was inescapable. She whimpered as the large, blunt head of the object demanded entrance. She was aware on some level of Trevor's husky voice uttering words of encouragement, of praise. Her breath was stuck in her throat, and it was hard to remember to inhale and exhale.

Ever so slowly, the foreign cock pressed deeper. The sensation of being completely filled was indescribable. The line between fiction and reality blurred, and in her mind she was the woman on the bed.

She panted, feeling the almost painful stretch as her body tried to accommodate the girth.

Trevor's voice commanded her attention. "Tilt your hips."

She did, and the cock slid a half inch deeper. Now it pressed a sensitive spot inside her sheath. She trembled violently as a rush of fiery heat built and bore down on her.

Trevor kissed her neck, letting his teeth sink into her sensitive skin. That twinge of pain almost triggered the imminent explosion. She tensed suddenly, afraid to let go with that obscene thing inside her. "Stop, Trevor."

He obeyed instantly.

Her breathing was so jerky it was hard to speak. "Enough. I want to watch another movie, please. But I need you to untie me."

Several seconds passed as she sensed his indecision. But he acceded to her request. He withdrew the toy, unbound her wrists, and, finally, took off the blindfold. As soon as she was free, she launched herself into his arms and began kissing him feverishly.

In fact, she practically knocked him off his feet. He'd been crouching at her side, and she nearly unbalanced them both.

She heard him chuckle roughly, and his arms came around her, holding her tight. She rained kisses all over his face, his neck, his chest.

She reached for his cock, but he stopped her. "No. I can't handle it. Believe me."

She licked his collarbone. "Then go put in another movie. One *you* like this time."

He released himself from her clinging arms with obvious reluctance and went back to the DVD player. When he turned around, the first flickering images on the screen lit up his face.

What she saw there made her stomach quiver. She held out her arms. "Come here. But take off the robe."

This time their positions were reversed. She cradled him in the vee of her thighs, and he rested his back against her breasts. She stroked his hair lightly as the movie began. His arms and shoulders were rigid. She massaged them gently until she felt him shift and finally relax into her embrace.

The story on the screen now appeared to be French. It opened with a young man cycling in the countryside. The day was hot, and he had abandoned his shirt. His chest and shoulders glistened with perspiration.

You could almost smell the scent of new-mown hay. Butterflies tumbled and circled over the verdant fields, and fluffy white clouds skidded across a deep blue sky. A well-known classical concerto played softly, but Dani couldn't quite place it.

The man spotted a river in the distance. You could hear his words of relief. He bumped down a rutted, dusty dirt path to where large stands of rushes guarded the edge of the water.

Without ceremony he stripped off his shoes, trousers, and briefs. He was tanned all over. His buttocks were tight and muscular, and his prick dangled heavily at his thigh. You could see the urgency in his motions, the almost palpable need for respite from the heat.

He parted the rushes with one long arm and froze. A few feet beyond where he stood, a woman bathed in the river. Her arms were lifted to the sky as she washed her long blond hair.

Her back was to him, but as she knelt and rinsed, he could see the curve of one plump breast tipped with a raspberry nipple.

"Mon Dieu."

Even Dani could translate that much.

Stealthily the man crept closer, slipping into the water with a barely perceptible splash. The woman was singing, and her lilting voice drowned out the man's silent approach.

She whirled at the last moment and he snatched her into his arms, covering her mouth with his and kissing her roughly. She flailed in his grasp, but he held her firmly. Her skin was pale against his darker body.

Dani touched Trevor's nipples lightly, and he jerked as if she had given him an electric shock.

She teased the shell of his ear with her tongue. "Relax," she muttered with naughty irony. "Just feel."

The man in the water lifted the woman's hips and slid her down onto his erection. Her head fell back, and her wet hair streamed toward the water.

Dani circled Trevor's cock with her right hand and squeezed it gently. She didn't move her hand beyond that. His fingers gripped her thighs.

On screen, the young man pumped fiercely, his face a mask of determination.

Suddenly, without warning, a second woman appeared, launching herself at him with a screech and trying to free her friend. The three grappled in the water, panting and struggling.

The man cursed in French and grabbed both of them around their waists. The huge muscles in his arms strained as he strode toward the bank, carrying his bounty. As he pushed through the high grass at a slightly different spot, he noticed the pleasant alfresco picnic laid out by the two friends.

He tumbled his original lover to her back and thrust between her legs, all the while keeping an iron grip on the second woman's wrist. When she beat at his back and tried to bite his arm, he shook her loose with superhuman strength.

As he roared in climax, the second woman knelt, spellbound, as she watched her friend climax as well. A crafty look came over her face, and she sprawled on her back beside them, fingering her pussy.

She spoke quietly to the man, and his head jerked in her direction. He reared to his knees, still hard, and fell on top of her. She wrapped her legs around his waist and took him deep, crying out in French as he began to fuck her.

Dani licked the back of Trevor's neck. She released his prick and with both hands cupped his balls. She pulled at them and kneaded them gently, brushing Trevor's erection in passing. She felt the tension in his body, accurately gauged his knife-edged arousal, but the appealing movie continued.

The three lovers fell into an exhausted doze beneath the hot summer sun. But the women were only feigning sleep, and when they realized the man was out for the count, they slipped from his side and grinned in silent complicity.

One of them used a knife to cut two thin strips from the square of white linen covering their loaf of bread. The second woman found two sturdy broken branches and, with her friend's help, drove them deep into the ground at the top edges of the quilt. They tied the man's wrists securely and bound him to the stakes.

Then they lay beside him and fondled each other's breasts lazily until he awoke. He called out in anger when he realized his predicament. The women laughed tauntingly and kissed each other briefly. Then the one he had screwed in the river delved into the picnic basket and pulled out a jar of honey.

The man's eyes widened in apprehension as she unscrewed the lid and used a silver spoon to scoop out a dollop of thick golden liquid. She dribbled it over each of his nipples and traced a line down his chest to his groin.

It took two spoonfuls to completely coat his thick, erect prick. When he was suitably covered, one woman attacked his nipples and the other started licking his cock. The camera zoomed in on the man's face, capturing his pained, pleasurable agony.

Dani touched Trevor's nipples lightly, rubbing the hard tips. She whispered in his ear, "It will be summer soon. We'll take a blanket out to the cliff top and I'll give you the honey treatment. Would you like that, my love?"

A great groan ripped from deep inside his chest. "God, yes." His mutter was barely audible, but the hunger in his voice made her ache.

Dani rubbed his chest as they watched the woman kneeling

between the helpless man's legs. The Frenchwoman sucked enthusiastically. He was so close to the edge you could feel it. His feet dug into the quilt. His back arched. . . .

Trevor bit out a curse and flipped over, dragging her down the seat until she lay flat on her back. His big body settled heavily between her legs, stretching her thighs wide.

"Trevor. The movie . . ."

"To hell with the movie."

He moved to take her, and she gasped out a protest. "Wait. I wanted to taste you."

He seemed blind and dumb to her protests. He lifted her legs to his shoulders and entered her roughly. She reached for the arms of the chair, trying to anchor herself. Her inner tissues were still sensitive from the intrusion of the toy earlier. Every slide of her husband's firm length stroked and shivered against her moist flesh. She tried to hold back, but her body hummed with searing pleasure.

She screamed and twisted beneath him, trying to claw her way inside his body. The long, torturous foreplay had sharpened her senses. Her climax slammed into her, stealing her breath. For a half second, blackness pressed in, and then she heard his shout and felt the hot spurt of his seed deep inside her. Over and over he came, until his wrenching orgasm seemed in danger of turning him inside out.

He slumped on top of her. Dani's body quivered and throbbed. The urgent need dipped only momentarily. The voices from the movie filled her head—the man's agonized moans, the women's little cries of delight.

Over Trevor's shoulder, her eyes focused blurrily on the screen. A close-up shot of the man's bound wrists sent a jolt of fire between her legs. Then came a view of the woman's plump ass rising and falling on a thick, veined penis.

Trevor was mumbling against her neck, his erection only momentarily diminished. He sucked deep, leaving a bruise she could feel. He reared to his knees, disconnecting their bodies and tumbling them both to the floor.

He grabbed handfuls of her hair and pulled her lips to his cock. She swallowed him deep, almost sobbing in her eagerness. Her skin actually hurt. Her pussy was an aching void.

Trevor quaked and shivered, talking to her in low, ragged cries. "Harder, Dani. Deeper."

His hands in her hair held her head in a vise. Her subservient position sparked a vision of the countess and her victim. She released Trevor and pulled free, wincing as strands of hair got caught in his fingers.

She shoved him to his back, taking him by surprise. She sat on his face, and this time she was the one to grab hanks of his hair. "Make me come."

He licked her greedily. She didn't last thirty seconds. A second powerful climax threw her over a crest, and before she could recover he was between her legs again, pinning her to the floor with the weight of his surging hips.

There was nothing to hang on to. She tumbled in waves of sensation, lost to reality. Trevor's hoarse groan signaled his release, and she peaked one last time before closing her eyes and helplessly giving in to the shining darkness.

Trevor could hear his heart beating in his ears. What he feared had happened. During the two movies, he had kept a tight rein on his reactions, anxious to monitor his wife's every mood. Her rising excitement made his own arousal sharper. He'd done everything he could to keep the situation under wraps, but feeling Dani's hands on his cock while watching the hapless male tormented in such a titillating fashion had done him in.

He lifted his weight to his arms, chagrined to feel how much his biceps quivered. Dani's eyes were closed, and his heart clenched in panic. He rolled off her and ran a tentative hand over her flat stomach. "Sweetheart. Talk to me."

Her lips moved, but he couldn't understand what she said. He leaned closer. Her lips grazed his stubbly jaw. "How many more of those movies do you have?" she asked in a slurred voice, a tiny smile tilting her lips.

His pulse slowed in relief. He slid two fingers inside her and palpated her G-spot. Dani whimpered, but didn't protest. He kissed her gently, easing his tongue into her mouth and probing, feeling half-crazed with a desire that wouldn't fade. "Wouldn't the more important question be: How many more movies can we watch and not fuck each other to death?" he asked huskily.

She caught his tongue and sucked on it. He cursed and worked her pussy rhythmically, dropping his head to her breast.

Her tits rose and fell as she took in a deep breath. "It's a definite possibility, Trevor. I suppose we'll have to ration ourselves to make them last."

He stroked her tummy, grinning to himself as he tongued her pretty navel. "Don't worry, angel. I won't run out." After all, sex films were easy enough to replace. But a woman like Dani came along once in a lifetime.

Elizabeth Scott enjoys hearing from readers.
She can be reached at lizybeth13@aol.com.